Illustrated HISTORY of Antarctica

Marcia Stenson

RANDOM HOUSE
NEW ZEALAND

National Library of New Zealand Cataloguing-in-Publication Data

Stenson, Marcia.
Illustrated history of Antarctica / Marcia Stenson.
Includes index.
ISBN 978-1-86941-924-0
1. Antarctica—History—Juvenile literature.
[1. Antarctica—History.] I. Title.
998.9—dc 22

A RANDOM HOUSE BOOK
published by
Random House New Zealand
18 Poland Road, Glenfield, Auckland, New Zealand
www.randomhouse.co.nz

First published 2007

ISBN 978 1 86941 924 0

Design: Sharon Grace, Grace Design, Auckland

Front cover illustration: (clockwise from top left): Edmund Hillary (S Mckay collection, Canterbury Museum); iceberg (Michael Van Woert, NOAA); Eric Philips (Alexander Colhoun, US Antarctic Program/National Science Foundation); Scott Base sign (Commander John Bortniak, NOAA); Australia Post; Emperor penguins (Michael Van Woert. NOAA)
Front and back cover background: Rob Suisted
Back cover illustration: killer whale (NOAA)

Printed in China by Everbest Printing Co Ltd

Contents

Introduction

Antarctica — the windiest, highest, driest, coldest place on earth

Antarctica, the last place on earth to be explored, as recently as the lifetime of our own grandparents or great grandparents, is now well known. Nearly all of its mountain regions have been explored or photographed from the air. Even areas under the ice have been mapped, using radio-echo sounding equipment.

Antarctica covers about 14,200,000 square kilometres. It is the fifth largest continent, about the size of Australia and Indonesia together. Its thick ice sheet lifts it to an average height of 4 kilometres above sea level. It is the highest of the continents.

- Antarctic means 'opposite to Arctic'. It is a continent surrounded by ocean. The great plateau is the most desolate, storm-driven place on earth, much colder than the Arctic.

- The Arctic is an ocean almost surrounded by continents. At the North Pole, land lies under 3 kilometres of ocean. The deep ocean only freezes on the surface. Plants and animals are different from those found in Antarctica: polar bears are only found in the Arctic, penguins only in Antarctica.

New Zealand and the Antarctic

New Zealand is one of Antarctica's closest neighbours and Antarctica has always been important to us. It is possible that early Polynesian sailors knew of the area. Some legends tell of huge icebergs in a frozen sea. New Zealand was also an important base for the first sailors who explored the Antarctic. Nowadays, many expeditions to Antarctica still leave from New Zealand.

The worst airline disaster in New Zealand history happened in Antarctica in 1979 when a DC-10 crashed on Mt Erebus, killing all aboard. It was said that everyone in New Zealand knew someone on that flight.

Antarctica is important to everyone in the world

Antarctica drives our weather, influencing both heat and sea levels. The thick ice cap of the high Polar Plateau and the glaciers reflect back 80% of the sun's heat, moderating the world's climate. Seventy per cent of the world's fresh water is locked up there. Algae from the melting glaciers feed krill, the basis of an important food chain.

A special presentation pack of New Zealand stamps issued in 1984 about research in Antarctica.

Antarctica's round shape is broken up by the Antarctic Peninsula and the two massive bays of the Ross and Weddell seas. South of the Antarctic Circle (at 66.6°S) the sun disappears altogether for four months of winter. But in summer the sun is seen for 24 hours a day. On 17 January 1773 Captain James Cook and the crews of the ships *Resolution* and *Adventure* were the first recorded people to cross this line.

The heroic exploits of Antarctic explorers are familiar to many New Zealanders. 'I am just going outside and may be some time,' said the severely frostbitten Captain Oates, before leaving the tent and going out to his death in a fierce storm, so that his companions would not be slowed down. Captain Oates was in charge of the expedition's horses.

The best place for scientists to check on the health of the planet

From Antarctica, scientists can monitor the ozone layer, carbon dioxide levels, and gather data about global warming and climate changes. Antarctica is the world's richest source of extraterrestrial matter; in other places on earth, human settlement makes meteorites more difficult to find. One Martian meteorite found in the Allan Hills in 1984 had plunged to earth about 15 million years ago.

- At the South Geographic Pole whichever way you stand, you face north.
- The Pole of Inaccessibility (85°S and 65°E), 3718 metres above sea level, is the centre of the continent: the point that is furthest away from all the coasts and hardest to get to.
- At the South Magnetic Pole a compass needle points straight down.

The ice plateau

Around the South Geographic Pole there is a vast, high plateau. Like runny icing on a cake, the ice slowly but steadily spills out and down through huge glaciers onto ice shelves. From these, large blocks or icebergs break off, floating northwards into the Pacific and Atlantic Oceans.

It is a dark, cold world in winter, with temperatures averaging from -50 to -60°C. Savage storms frequently rage across the continent. In mid-August the sun begins to show above the horizon and when the pack ice breaks up in November, birds, seals, whales, and scientists return for the summer season.

Mt Erebus (3794 metres) is the most active of the volcanoes in Antarctica.

- The Point of Safe Return (PSR) is 3200 kilometres from Christchurch on the way to McMurdo Sound. Before the PSR pilots could still abort the flight and have enough fuel to return. After passing the PSR they have to land in Antarctica, even if that means doing so into the teeth of a storm — and in Antarctica the weather can turn very nasty, very quickly.

- What time is it at the Pole? All time zones meet at the Pole. Most Antarctic bases run on their home time but American bases run on New Zealand time because they fly in and out of New Zealand.

- For the Antarctic Treaty, the boundary of Antarctica lies at 60°S latitude.

Key Points

1. The Antarctic is a continent, the Arctic is an ocean.
2. The Antarctic is the coldest, windiest, highest, driest place on earth.
3. It was the last place on earth to be explored.
4. There are three poles: the South Geographic, the South Magnetic and the Pole of Inaccessibility.
5. The Antarctic is very important to humans because it moderates our climate.

Where evidence comes from

How do historians find out about Antarctica's past? No humans have ever lived in Antarctica, so no archaeological evidence exists. Although Polynesian legends tell of a vast Southern Ocean with frozen seas, there is no evidence to show that they ever landed or settled there.

The French explorer, Dumont D'Urville published an account of his voyage in 1842.

Written records

The first human visitors often made notes of their findings. Captains, like James Cook, kept records of their voyages in ship's logs. Diaries of explorers, like Robert Falcon Scott, and autobiographies, like Edmund Hillary's own version of his journey to the Pole, help us understand Antarctica.

But diaries can be unreliable. Explorers, half-starved, cooped up in tiny tents in terrible weather, often make bitter and twisted comments about their companions. If they survive, they are often good friends again. Captain Oates said in one of his letters home: 'Please remember that when a man is having a hard time he says things about other people which he would regret afterwards.' One explorer said of his diary that it acted as a Father Confessor for him. By making notes, he got rid of his anger, tiredness and depression. Diaries give us clues, but have to be treated carefully.

Other sorts of written records are also not foolproof and ship's logs can go missing. We need to check against other evidence. Artefacts such as the historic huts built by explorers are useful.

Scientific records made over the years have helped us learn about the ancient geological history of the continent.

Fossils

On Captain Scott's expedition to the Pole, the scientist E.A.Wilson collected rock samples from the Beardmore Glacier. Embedded in the samples were fern-like fossil leaves. Even

Ernest Shackleton's hut at Cape Royds, Ross Island, gets a new roof in 2006. Historic huts help us understand the past.

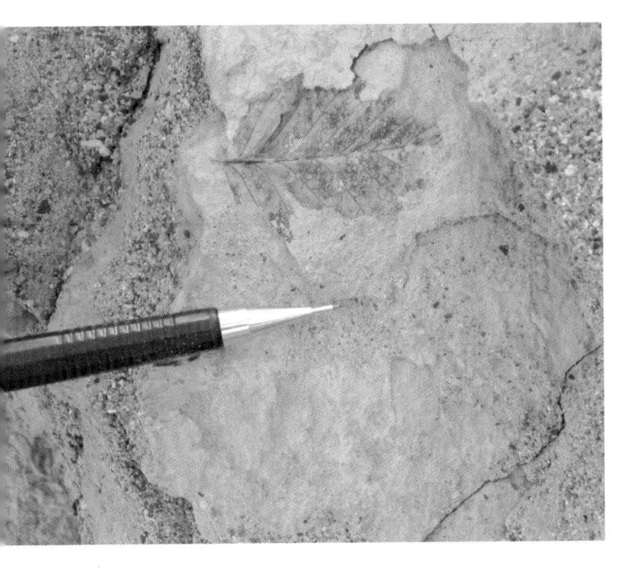

Fossils of ancient plants and animals are found embedded in rocks.

though Scott's party was struggling to survive, they carried 14 kilograms of rock samples over 640 kilometres on their sledge. The fossils were later found with their dead bodies. One of Wilson's ancient leaf fossils was later found to be *Glossopteris*, a plant from the ancient southern hemisphere continent. This provided the first proof that Antarctica was once part of the ancient supercontinent of Gondwanaland.

Samples from the deep ice and the sea floor

Scientists are able to drill ice cores and samples of other material from well below the surface of the continent. Using these samples, they can deduce what happened in the past in Antarctica. But, as with written records, interpreting scientific evidence can be difficult.

The best idea is to use a range of evidence, but always be ready to rethink our conclusions if new evidence comes up or if the interpretation changes.

Key Points

Evidence about the past of Antarctica comes from:

1. Written records, such as ship's logs, diaries and autobiographies.
2. Artefacts, such as the historic huts.
3. Scientific Evidence, such as fossils and ice cores.

There is no archaeological evidence because humans have never lived there.

Antarctica: the continent

The ancient supercontinent

In the very ancient history of the world there was once a supercontinent that scientists have called Gondwanaland. About 183 million years ago, after violent eruptions, this giant land mass began to break up and drift slowly to the corners of the globe. Evidence for this supercontinent and its break-up was found in Antarctica. In the 1960s, geologists matched up sediments layered in Antarctica 280 million years ago with those in other continents. In both places they found the same types of fossils, of species quite unable to cross oceans, supporting the idea that these continents had once been joined together.

Ice

Antarctica is the largest block of ice on earth. Almost 98% of Antarctica is covered in a vast ice sheet that has built up over millions of years as loose snow crystals have gradually compacted down into ice.

180 million years ago, Antarctica had plains, rivers, swamps and vegetation. Fossils in ice and sediment core samples show that conifer and beech tree forests grew in the Antarctic only two million years ago. Forty million years ago, Australia and New Zealand broke away. South America broke off 23 million years ago. When a deep sea channel cut Antarctica off from warm water and weather, the climate grew colder. The once fertile land moved into an ice age. To survive in the bitter cold, plants and animals became highly specialised.

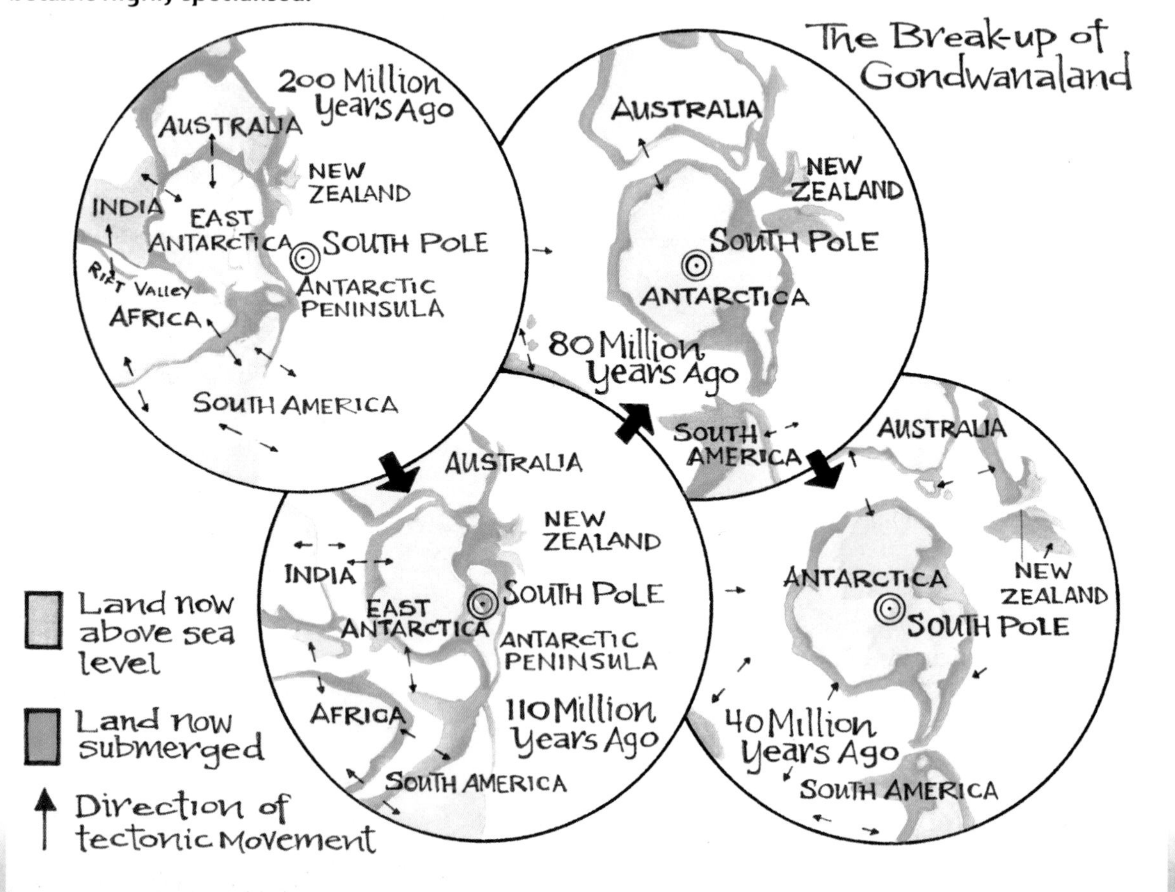

The Geographic Pole is 2835 metres above sea level. The marker, itself, is 4 metres high.

Ice sheets retreat or advance depending on how much radiation they get from the sun. At times in the past the ice has covered a far greater area than now. At other times the ice has retreated much more. At the South Pole itself, the ice sheet is nearly 3 kilometres thick. The ice cover moves slowly but steadily down from the Polar Plateau towards the sea. Giant streams of ice drain the interior ice shelves and feed huge icebergs into the coastal seas.

- The thickest ice is in a subglacial trench 400 kilometres from the Terre Adélie coast and is 4776 metres deep (half the height of Mt Everest).

- With the sun at a much lower angle, polar regions receive less radiation and heat than the tropics. They also reflect more solar radiation. Polar Regions have less dust and water vapour in their atmosphere and only trap a small amount of the sun's heat.

- Averaging 2300 metres above sea level, Antarctica is the highest of the continents. Most of this is ice. With no ice, it would only be 500 metres above sea level. Antarctica is also the lowest continent. The Bentley subglacial trench is 2539 metres below sea level.

The South Geographic Pole

If you think of the world as a chunky spinning top, the South Geographic Pole is its bottom point. It is the southern end of the axis around which the world spins.

The Pole is in the middle of the Polar Plateau. While the Pole always stays in the same place, the thick ice sheet of the Plateau moves about 9 metres a year. Today's ice at the Pole will reach the coast in about 120,000 years. This means that the South Pole marker has to be shifted every year. A Global Positioning System (GPS) uses satellites to fix its position.

The Antarctic Circle

The South Magnetic Pole is the southern point of the earth's magnetic field.

The Polar Plateau is one big glacier, over 2000 metres thick, flowing down on all sides from the Pole over a descending series of plateaus. Its thousands of kilometres of flat, snow-covered ice extends over most of East Antarctica. It is very cold and dry.

The Transantarctic Mountains separate East and West Antarctica. They are 3200 kilometres in length and reach 4897 metres above sea level. At either end of the mountain chain are two large basins.

❄ Latitude and Longitude: As soon as sailors went out of sight of land they used latitude and longitude to work out where they were on the world's surface. Latitude starts from the Equator (0˚), an imaginary line running all the way around the very middle of the world. Imaginary lines of latitude divide the area from the Equator to each of the Poles (90˚) into degrees. New

The Antarctic Continent is the most isolated continent on the globe. It is 950 kilometres from South America, 2200 from New Zealand, 2300 from Tasmania and 3600 from Australia.

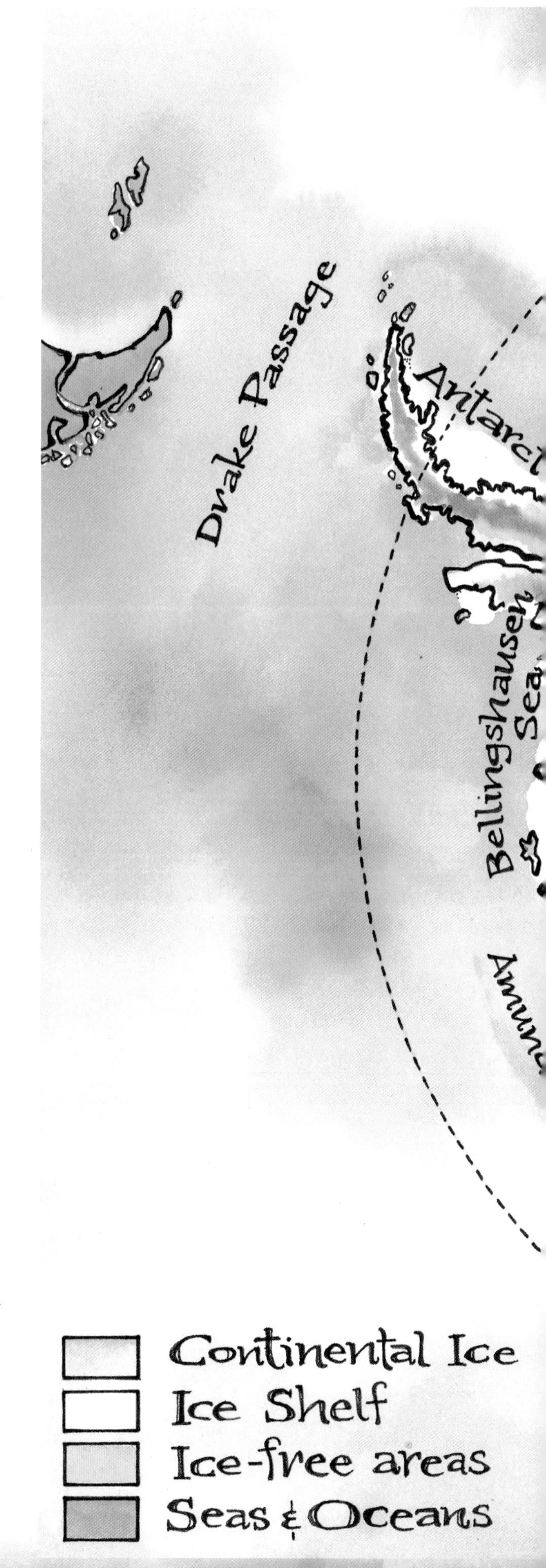

Antarctic Circle
Weddell Sea
East Antarctica
Shackleton Range
Pole of Relative Inaccessibility
3720m
South Pole
2800m
West Antarctica
Trans Antarctic Mountains
Polar Plateau
Shackleton Gl.
Beardmore Gl.
Nimrod Gl.
Ross Ice Shelf
Mt Erebus
3794m
Dry Valleys
Ross Sea
Southern Ocean
South Magnetic Pole
Cape Denison
0
1000km

Zealand lies between latitudes 34° and 48° South of the Equator. Great Britain lies between 50° and 60° North of the Equator. Longitude is also measured in degrees East and West from the Greenwich Meridian, an imaginary line running from the North Pole to the South Pole through the town of Greenwich in England. Using minutes as well gives a more exact position (60 minutes = 1 degree).

- A glacier is a river of ice moving slowly but steadily down to the sea. Of Antarctica's many glaciers, the Beardmore is one of the largest, at 200 kilometres long. It flows north into the Ross Ice Shelf.

- Icebergs are formed when a section of ice breaks off the end of a glacier and goes into the sea. This is called 'calving'. It is spectacular. Kilometres of ice can suddenly crumble away, with clouds of 'ice smoke'. Many icebergs stay close to the continent for years. Others drift north, breaking up and melting as they go.

- Crevasses: As the ice in a glacier flows slowly but steadily downhill it meets obstacles, like narrow valleys, ridges or rocks. The great pressure on the ice twists and forces it out of shape. Great fissures appear, sometimes suddenly opening up with a crack like a rifle shot. These crevasses can be a few centimetres wide or wide enough to swallow a ship twice over. They can be formed along the glacier or across the glacier. When they become covered with snow, you cannot see the crevasse and the thin snow bridges that have formed across the top of the opening can collapse with your weight. Travel over the ice becomes very dangerous. The sheer blue walls of a crevasse can be 36 metres or more in depth.

Climate and weather

Blizzards: Gale-force winds can rise to speeds of 150 kilometres per hour with gusts of up to 190 kilometres. They may last for days. The

The Ross Ice Shelf has a cliff front which ranges from 15–50 metres high. It is the world's largest body of floating ice. About the size of Texas, it is bigger than France and almost all afloat. It is a vast, triangular-shaped raft of ice that is flexible and loosely attached to the land. From the air it looks like a flat plain, but it is full of crevasses. Where it meets the land it can be up to 1000 metres thick. It is fed by five ice streams and seven major glaciers. These glaciers push the whole sheet north at about a metre each day.

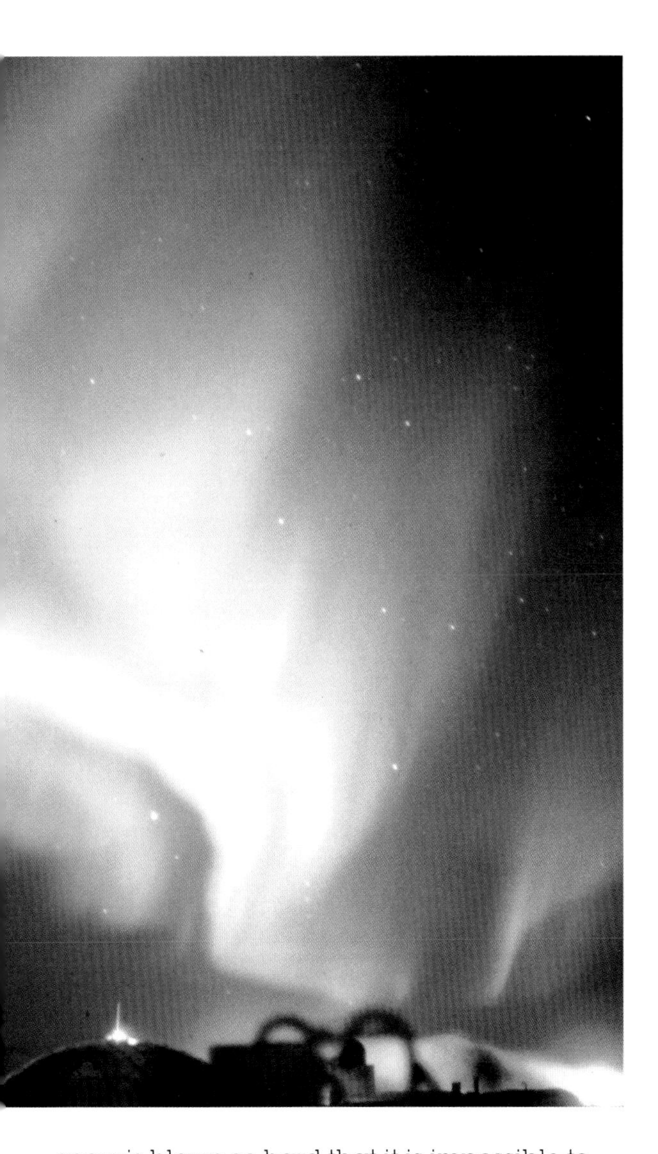

Aurora Australis: One of the most spectacular phenomena in Antarctica is the Aurora or southern lights. To Maori it is known as *Tahu-nui-a-rangi*, literally, the great burning in the sky. It is created by charged particles high in the atmosphere.

snow is blown so hard that it is impossible to see things an arm's length away. Everything not very securely tied down gets blown away.
Katabatic Winds: These are powerful winds that roll downhill from the high Polar Plateau, gathering speed as they come. They can reach speeds of around 300 kilometres per hour. They may begin as a breeze at the Pole, but by the time the cold, dense air reaches the glaciers it is at full speed and power.
Cold: It is so cold in midwinter that if a cup of boiling water is thrown in the air it will snap freeze before it hits the ground. In these conditions, human skin sticks to metal. Wind chill is the biggest danger for humans. The earth's coldest temperature, -91 °C, was recorded in 1997 at Vostok Station. The mean annual temperature of the Polar Plateau is -57 °C.

Dry: Antarctica is really the world's largest desert. Low temperatures mean that air masses can hold very little water vapour. There is no rain in the interior and only a small amount of snow is carried there by the wind.
The Dry Valleys: These are ancient polar deserts of rock, gravel and ice. Cold, dry winds blow through the valleys. Over summer, the rock absorbs heat, which evaporates any snow that may have fallen in winter. For the last two million years not much snow (or rain) has fallen there, and strong winds blow away what little there is. The Dry Valleys form about 2% of Antarctica and are important for science, as fossils are often found there.

- Lakes are mainly found in the Dry Valleys. In the past there were more lakes in the mountains. Most have a permanent cover of ice, 2–5 metres thick. This melts around the shoreline in summer. Some are freshwater lakes and some are salty.

Antarctica's permanent residents

Humans are recent visitors. The permanent residents of Antarctica are lichens, algae, birds and animals.

The 300–400 species of lichens are often found in rocks in the Dry Valleys. They can photosynthesise even when frozen at very low temperatures. They are not separate plants but a combination of algae or cyanobacteria and a fungus living together. They grow very slowly. On the Antarctic peninsula or the islands they will grow 1 centimetre in 100 years but in the Dry Valleys, they take 1000 years to grow

Scientists at work mapping the Dry Valleys and describing the rocks.

1 centimetre. They can live for at least 2000 years.

Algae are simple plant organisms and many species are found in Antarctica. Phytoplankton live on the surface of the ocean. Cryoplankton live and reproduce in snow banks and glaciers. Sometimes patches of red or green coloured algae will be found in summer near the Antarctic Coast. These are called 'Red Snow'. Algae are also found in meltwater pools in summer and in colonies at the bottom of freshwater lakes.

The Antarctic's animals include corals, sea anemones, krill, squid and vertebrates such as birds, fish and whales.

Key Points

1. Antarctica once was part of Gondwanaland, a fertile land with trees, lush vegetation and animals.
2. Antarctica is the largest block of ice on the planet.
3. The ice moves slowly but steadily towards the sea.
4. Antarctica is very cold and dry.
5. Humans are visitors to Antarctica; the permanent residents are lichens, algae, birds and sea animals.

Orange lichen covers rocks on the Antarctic Peninsula.

The Southern Ocean and subantarctic islands

The Southern Ocean is a wild and stormy place. In a vast ocean with no land to stop them, huge swells can form and grow. Sailors have reported waves as high as 5 or 6 storey buildings coming towards them at 65 kilometres per hour. Sometimes the top two or three storeys will collapse. The winds are fierce. In 1912 the *Aurora* was steaming at full speed into the wind, and the crew saw the wake of the ship flowing back from the bow.

Huge icebergs, formed when ice breaks off or 'calves' from the Antarctic ice sheet, are common in the Southern Ocean. The largest ever recorded was over 160 kilometres long. Small ones are called 'growlers'. They float northwards into the open ocean, occasionally being seen off New Zealand's South Island coast (this happened most recently in November–December 2006).

Shipwrecks were common in the Subantarctic Islands. This is an artist's version of the wreck of the *General Grant* in the Auckland Islands in 1866.

Sailors named the stormy sea areas the Roaring Forties (between 40˚S and 50˚S), the Furious Fifties (between 50˚S and 60˚S) and the Screaming Sixties (between 60˚S and 70˚S). Wild winds, horrifying storms and massive seas shipwrecked and drowned many sailors.

Subantarctic islands

These are scattered, isolated islands that lie between latitudes 47°S and 60°S. They are frequently battered by the storms and gales of the Roaring Forties. Because they are surrounded by the warmer ocean they do not have permanent snow or ice, but have lots of rain and sleet instead.

❄ In the Auckland Islands, the wind is often strong enough to blow falling spray back up the steep cliffs in a kind of upside-down waterfall.

Some have deep fiords and lakes created by ancient glaciers; others have craters from extinct volcanoes. Those closest to New Zealand and Australia include the Snares, Bounty, Antipodes, Auckland, Campbell and Macquarie islands. Sealers had temporary camps in these islands. Shipwrecks on their stormy coasts were so common that many have shelters for castaways.

The four main islands of the Auckland Islands (New Zealand) are Adams, Auckland, Disappointment and Enderby, and were formed by old volcanoes. Their sheer cliffs, rippled by old lava flows, tower up to 300 metres high. There are two large, well protected harbours on Auckland Island. Maori once camped there and a Pakeha settlement was tried on Enderby in 1849 but abandoned several years later. There were also two sheep farms that did not succeed. The New Zealand government declared the Auckland Islands a nature reserve in 1934.

The Auckland Islands are a graveyard for ships. At least eight have been wrecked and more than 100 lives lost. New Zealand government representatives used to go every year to check the huts and supplies they had set up for shipwrecked sailors. In 1999, the yacht *Totorore* was lost with no survivors.

❄ The *General Grant* was sailing from Melbourne to London laden with gold bullion when she crashed into the towering cliffs of the main island early in the morning on 14 May 1866. She drifted into a sea cave where the roof forced the masts through the hull and there she sank. Only 15 out of the 83 on board survived. Four were lost trying to sail a small boat to Bluff to get help. The rest spent 18 months struggling to survive on the island before they were rescued. Treasure seekers have tried to salvage the gold from the *General Grant*, but they have all failed.

Campbell Island (New Zealand) is an extinct volcano covered in tussock. It was discovered in 1814 by Captain Frederick Hasselborough in the ship *Perseverance*. The island had a whaling station from 1909 to 1916, and 60 Southern Right Whales were killed there. Farming was more successful here than on the Auckland Islands but ended in 1931 when 4000 sheep and a few cattle were left to run wild. It became a reserve in 1954 and in 1990 the last wild sheep were removed.

Macquarie Island (Australia) is halfway between Tasmania and the Antarctic. It is a narrow tussock-covered ridge of land, charted and named by Hasselborough in the *Perseverance* in 1810. He reported seeing a shipwreck off the coast. Macquarie is the only place where hot magma from the earth's mantle is pushed to the surface, causing

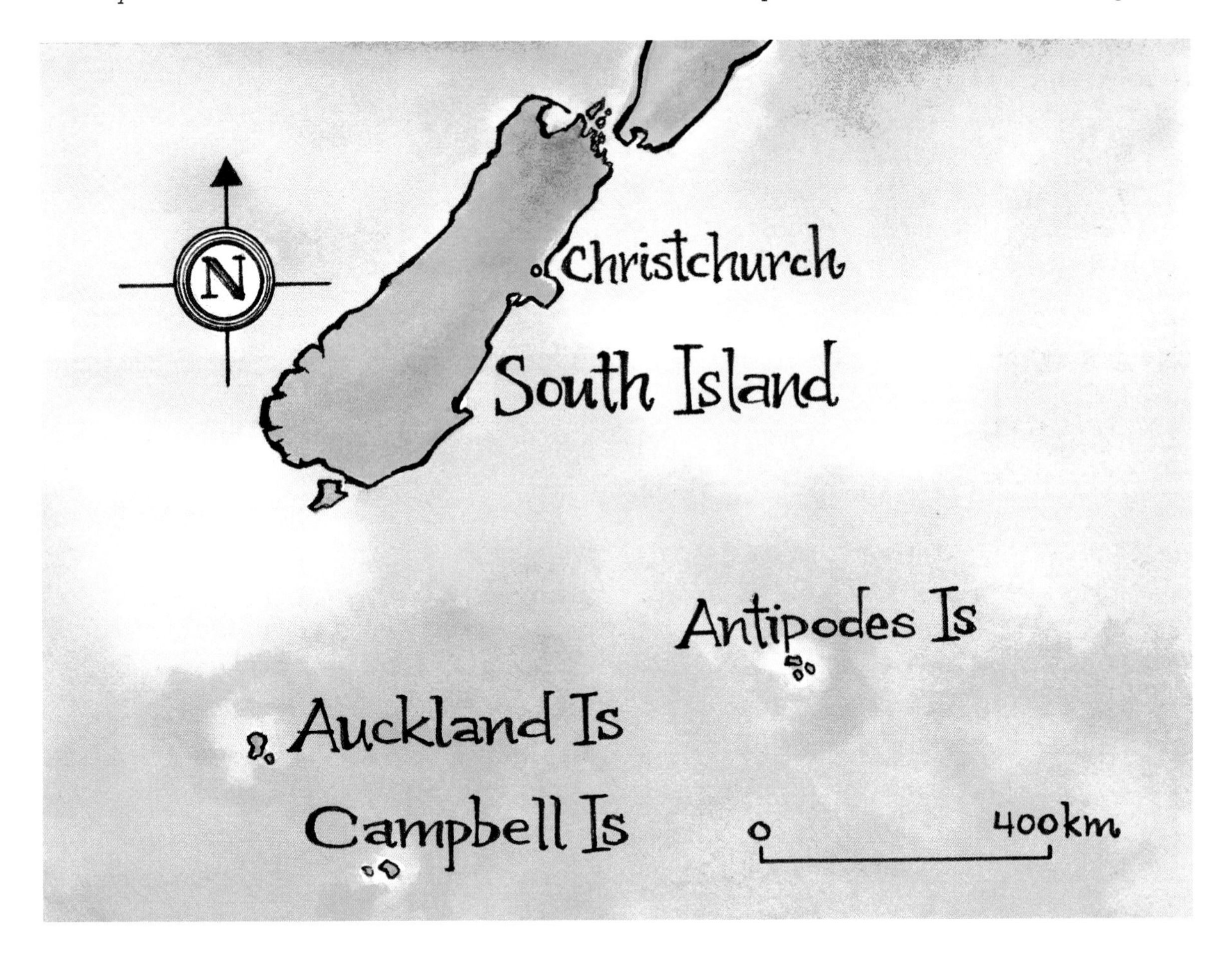

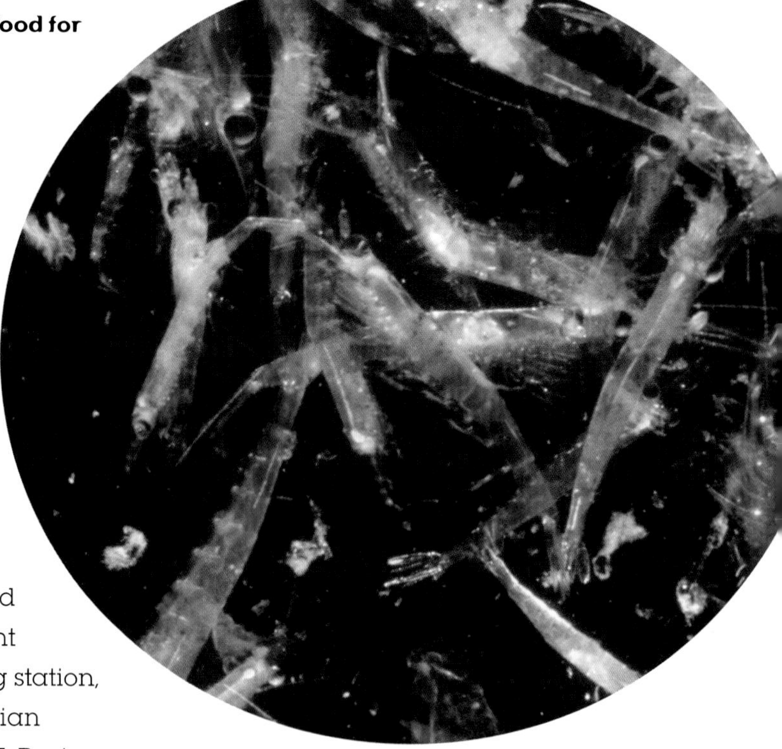

Krill, seen magnified here, are the basic food for many animals in the Antarctic Ocean.

regular earthquakes, mud slides and rock falls. The island is very windy and wet. Sealers killed seals and penguins for oil and fur seal skins there. It became a wildlife sanctuary in 1933 and today has an Australian scientific station on it.

Glaciers cover 60% of the mountainous island of South Georgia (Britain), which was first sighted in 1675 by an English merchant, Anthony de la Roche. Captain Cook landed in 1775 and claimed it for Britain. It was an important sealing base. The first Antarctic whaling station, Grytviken, was set up here by a Norwegian company operating from 1904 until 1965. During the 1982 war between Britain and Argentina, South Georgia was captured by Argentina and then recaptured by the British.

What lives in the Southern Ocean?

Many of the subantarctic islands have big bird populations. The vegetation is often lush and green with grasses, flowering plants, lichens, mosses, fungi and giant kelp. The tussock cover gives good shelter for birds. The world's largest population of wandering albatrosses lives on the Auckland Islands, together with mollymawks, yellow-eyed penguins and Hooker's sea lions. Seal and penguin populations are rapidly recovering from the devastation of being killed for oil. Introduced animals such as rats, rabbits, pigs and goats have become a problem. Rats eat birds' eggs. Rabbits, pigs and goats graze and destroy fragile plant species.

In the Antarctic Circle

Sea temperatures are low but do not change much between summer and winter. In McMurdo Sound the sea is usually about 1.9°C. Sea creatures grow slowly in such cold water and cold-blooded fish have developed their own anti-freeze, which prevents ice crystals growing in their blood.

The food chain

The area where cold Antarctic water mixes with warmer water from the Atlantic, Indian and Pacific oceans is called the Antarctic Convergence. It lies between latitudes 48˚S and 60˚S and is a very rich feeding ground for sea life. Here algae, fed from the guano of millions of birds, is released from the melting ice to bloom in the summer light and warmth.

Krill, among the world's most abundant animals, live on the algae in the ocean and are, in turn, the main food for whales, fish, birds, seals and penguins. Krill is a Norwegian word meaning 'small fry' and there are about 85 species of these tiny shrimp-like creatures. They can swim forwards and backwards, spawn in summer and live about five to ten years. Krill are found in dense concentrations and each one is nearly 50% protein — no wonder krill is called the power lunch of the Antarctic.

An Adélie penguin walks near the edge of the sea ice as a minke whale breaks the surface. Both are eaters of krill.

Among the krill-eaters are:

Penguins

Penguins are birds that have adapted to living 80% of the time in the ocean.

❄ Penguin fossils as old as 40,000,000 years have been found — including some fossils of a species as tall as humans. Penguins evolved from birds that could both swim and fly, but today all species have lost the ability to fly.

Penguins are warm blooded and are like tiny torpedoes in the water. They eat crustaceans, squid and fish and are eaten, in turn, by killer whales, leopard seals and Hooker's sea lions, and, in warmer waters, sharks. They breed in huge coastal colonies (some Adélie rookeries are estimated at about a million birds) and during the 13 weeks of the breeding season, the parents supply about 30 kilograms of feed for each chick. Humans have always liked them for their quirky behaviour.

❄ Seven out of 18 species are Antarctic or subantarctic. Both Adélie and emperor penguins breed on the Antarctic Continent. Chinstrap, gentoo and macaroni penguins (the latter named after a hairstyle because of the crest of orange plumes that sweep back over the bird's head) breed on the

Emperor penguins.

Above: With their spotted coats, long slender bodies and massive jaws, from a distance leopard seals look like sea serpents. They live in the pack ice but do travel north. They eat penguins, pups of other seals, fish, squid and krill. In turn, they get eaten by killer whales. If they can avoid this, they live for about 25 years.

A skua flies over Antarctica. It lives the furthest south of any bird and feeds on penguin eggs, chicks, fish and krill.

Subantarctic Islands and the Antarctic Peninsula. The king and rockhopper penguins breed only in the subantarctic zone. The royal penguin is only found on Macquarie Island.

❄ Emperor penguins can dive to around 300 metres and stay below for up to 18 minutes. As the only penguins to stay put in the Antarctic all year round, they have to incubate their eggs in winter. This is the father's job. He balances the single egg on the top of his feet and covers it with a fold of warm skin. He can handle up to -48°C because he has a double layer of high-density feathers. The penguins go into a dense huddle (10 birds to a square metre), with sometimes as many as 5000 birds in the group. The huddle is always on the move. Birds on the windy side slowly edge their way round to the sheltered side and then into the middle. As the whole group keeps moving, they end up back on the windy side and start again.

Seals

Fur seals and crabeater seals also eat krill.

Whales

Most whales, such as the humpback and the minke, are summer visitors to the Antarctic. They feed on small fish and krill and are still targets for commercial whalers. The whale population has increased in recent times, but is still much smaller than it was before commercial whaling began.

Birds

Shearwaters, albatrosses and skuas also live in Antarctica.

Below: Killer whales (*Orcinus orca*) with their bold black and white markings are the biggest of the dolphin family. Their high triangular fins stand a metre or more out of the water. The largest can be nearly 9 metres long, with a metre-wide mouth. They hunt in packs, sometimes smashing through thin ice to take seals and penguins off sheet ice. They are thought to breed in the waters surrounding Antarctica. This one is looking for a penguin for lunch.

Key Points

1. The Southern Ocean is a vast, wild and stormy area.
2. The subantarctic islands are isolated, battered by winds and rain, but mostly free of ice.
3. Krill are tiny sea creatures that play an important part in the food chain.
4. Birds, penguins, seals, whales and fish are all inhabitants of the Southern Ocean.
5. The fishing and conservation of fish stocks is a big issue in the Southern Ocean.

Human footprints

No humans have ever lived permanently in Antarctica; the environment is too unfriendly. For humans, the chief danger is wind chill. Fierce winds — so strong that the land appears to be boiling with snow — can cause frostbite in seconds. Each knot of wind has the effect of a drop of one degree in temperature on human skin and in very low temperatures human teeth can crack from the cold, dry air. Then there are the deep crevasses or masked holes of death. One false step, and death waits at the bottom of a long, long drop. Memorials and cairns remind us of those who have tried to challenge Antarctica and failed.

Explorers had reached every part of the world except Antarctica by the mid-nineteenth century. Modern inventions like the primus allowed explorers to reach the far south.

Sledging rations for one man for one day.

What to eat

Diet has been a major problem for human visitors. Explorers who wintered over near the coast ate seals, penguins and fish, but as soon as they moved inland they suffered from scurvy, caused by a shortage of fresh food. Eating huskies and ponies seemed to prevent scurvy, but those who ate dog livers suffered Vitamin A poisoning. They also needed high calorie diets — especially if they were pulling sledges. On early expeditions explorers were often close to starvation. Dehydration is also a danger in such a dry environment and explorers had to carry plenty of fuel so that they could melt the snow and ice needed for drinks.

❄ A sledging party took only highly concentrated foods, with the smallest possible daily ration in order to cut down on weight. The following list is the daily ration for a sledging man from Douglas

in Antarctica

Robert Falcon Scott's Hut Point shelter.

Mawson's 1912–13 sledging party: plasmon biscuit 340 g (biscuit made of wholemeal flour and milk powder) pemmican 227 g (powdered dried beef plus 50% beef fat); 57 g butter (high heat value, and very popular); 57 g chocolate; 142 g dried milk; 113 g sugar; 28 g cocoa; 7 g tea (cocoa used for the first and last meals of the day, tea for lunch); total 971 g. The dogs ate dried seal steaks with a little blubber added.

Other equipment for explorers included:

- Fur boots, called finnesko, made of reindeer skin with the fur outside.
- Tents modified to cope with wind. These were made in a circular pattern with a flounce at the bottom like the brim of a hat. Blocks of snow were put on the flounce to anchor the tent down.
- Sledging harnesses for both men and dogs. The harness was attached to the sledge. If you went down a crevasse your life would depend on the harness.

The earliest explorers built huts to provide shelter while they sat out the winter conditions. The oldest huts in Antarctica are those built by British Antarctic expeditions at Cape Adare. Ross Island has three huts: at Hut Point, Cape Evans and Cape Royds. On the Antarctic Peninsula, the oldest huts date back to the Swedish South Polar Expedition. They left behind shelters at Hope Bay, Paulet Island and

A British expedition party visiting a Norwegian tent sometime between 1910 and 1912.

Snow Hill Island. In the subantarctic islands there are old buildings left behind by sealers and castaways from shipwrecks. There are several huts still standing at Cape Denison from the 1911-14 Australasian Expedition. Most of these were prefabricated. Modern huts are flown in by helicopter.

At the South Pole

The first evidence of humans at the South Geographic Pole was a black tent and a Norwegian flag left by Roald Amundsen on 14 December 1911. Then, four weeks later (18 January 1912), Robert Scott and his party left the British flag there. As their contribution to the 1957 Geophysical Year, Americans established a station at the Pole. When Admiral George Dufek of the US Navy landed to inspect the site, he was the first person there since Captain Scott. The station became dangerous when it was crushed under snowdrifts and was replaced in 1975 by an aluminium geodesic dome 18 metres high.

Other Bases

By the 1970s, ten nations were operating 43 stations in Antarctica. Australia has three permanent stations — Mawson, Davis and Casey — and one on Macquarie Island. Mawson Base is the oldest continuously operating research

New Zealand's Scott Base is on Ross Island.

station south of the Antarctic Circle. New Zealand established Scott Base in 1957. Russia (USSR) set up Vostok Base in 1957 at the coldest inhabited place on earth. Another Russian station is Novolazarevskaya (1961), where a Russian surgeon once removed his own appendix.

The Amundsen-Scott South Pole station.

How have humans affected the environment?

We know that humans have introduced alien species such as dogs and ponies to Antarctica, as well as rats, goats and other animals and plants to the subantarctic islands, but damage has also been done in other ways.

Rubbish

The rubbish and waste left in Antarctica by human visitors decays very slowly in the dry climate. Until recently, scientific bases would burn waste or dump it in the sea, and sewage went straight into the sea. Iron and wood left over from building projects, too expensive to move, lay around the bases, while old machinery stood about dripping oil. Empty containers, glass, plastic and chemical waste were thrown over cliffs or down crevasses. Most bases, littered with empty fuel barrels and abandoned trucks, looked like toxic rubbish dumps.

After Greenpeace exposed this state of affairs in 1987, efforts were made to take rubbish home or recycle it. In 1989, the American base at McMurdo began a clean-up costing US$30,000,000. Thousands of oil drums, solvents, old transformers, asbestos, explosives and chemicals were removed. Most bases began to treat their sewage before discharging it. Many bases now have environmental officers to train staff and visitors to take more care.

Local residents

Penguins have been pushed out to make way for humans. In 1957, when Hallett Station was built by a joint USA and NZ operation, 6000 birds were shifted out of their rookery. After the station was destroyed by fire in 1964, the penguins slowly began recolonising the area. When France built an airstrip near their

Norwegian explorer and first man to the South Pole, Roald Amundsen, used dog teams very effectively in his 1911–12 expedition.

Dogs in the Antarctic

The thick hides of Arctic-bred sledge dogs or huskies were well suited to Antarctic conditions, and they were strong — able to haul great loads through high winds and blizzards, twice as fast as men. Four to six pairs of dogs were harnessed together with one lead dog in front, and the driver would stand on the back of the sledge and yell instructions. An experienced dog team would instinctively weave around obstacles. But they presented some difficulties too: at times dogs fought each other viciously and the driver would have to untangle the overturned sledge with a team of barking, fighting dogs attached.

The down side for the dogs was that they were often killed, either to feed the explorers or to feed other, stronger, dogs. Many were killed in crevasses. Antarctic Treaty nations decided that they should be removed from Antarctica for environmental reasons by 1994.

Dumont d'Urville Base in Terre Adélie, they damaged the animal and plant life and displaced an Adélie penguin colony.

Pollution

Oil spills have also affected the wildlife. In 1989, an Argentinean resupply ship, the *Bahia Paraiso,* sank near Palmer Station on the Antarctic Peninsula. More than 681,900 litres of fuel spilt into the ocean, with oil slicks covering some 100 square kilometres. About 30,000 penguins were affected because the accident happened when adult penguins were foraging at sea for their young.

Nuclear contamination

In March 1962, the USA began operating a 1.8 megawatt pressurised-water nuclear power plant, named 'Nukey Poo', at McMurdo station. The reactor leaked coolant water and the area was contaminated with radioactive material. A big clean-up took three years. The US Navy shipped back around 800 tonnes of radioactive junk and another 12,200 tonnes of earth and gravel to the USA for disposal.

Right: The American Antarctic Fire Department responds to an imaginary fuel spill as part of one of their practice drills.

A British Antarctic Survey sled dog team in 1965.

Key Points

1. Antarctica can be dangerous for humans.
2. Humans have built shelters and scientific bases in Antarctica.
3. Humans have introduced destructive alien species to Antarctica and to the subantarctic islands.
4. Humans have damaged the environment in Antarctica with their rubbish and pollution, and by displacing the residents.

The first humans

Polynesian navigators may have sailed into the Southern Ocean, but there is no evidence that humans reached Antarctica before the 1820s. Polynesian traditions tell of ice-covered oceans to the south. According to one legend, a navigator, Ui-te Rangiora, set out from Fiji in his canoe called Te Iwi-o-Atea for the island of Rapa but was blown south until the ocean was covered with white powder and great white rocks rose high in the sky.

Although they never travelled there, ancient Greeks were also interested in the Antarctic. They had named the constellation of stars above the North Pole *arctos* (bear), and later they dubbed the South Pole region as 'opposite the bear' or *anti-arctos*. The famous Greek philosopher Aristotle thought that the northern land mass of Eurasia must be balanced by some as yet undiscovered southern continent, which he called *Antarktos*. In AD 150, Ptolemy, a Greek geographer, felt there had to be a Terra Australis to balance the northern continents.

How Europeans saw the Pacific in 1570 after Spanish

Explorers from Europe

Europeans took the idea of an unknown southern continent from the Greeks. When sailors discovered new southern islands, they thought they had found parts of the great unknown southern continent.

Some of the earliest explorers of southern areas:

1578 Francis Drake, the English explorer, was the first recorded European to sail in southern seas, and discovered Cape Horn.

1622 Dirck Gerritsz Keyser, a Dutch pilot, driven off his course to 64°S, sighted snow-covered mountains, probably the South Shetland Islands.

in the Antarctic

explorers made discoveries and after Ferdinand Magellan circumnavigated the world in 1519–22.

Captain James Cook's ship, the *Resolution*, in the Antarctic in 1773.

1675 London merchant, Antonio de la Roché, attempting to round Cape Horn, sighted an Antarctic island to the south of latitude 54°.

1699 English astronomer Edmond Halley, sent south to seek unknown lands, conducted a survey of magnetic variation. He got almost as far as South Georgia.

1722 Frenchman Yves Joseph de Kerguelen-Tremarec discovered the Kerguelen Islands south of 49°. He returned with tales of a paradise. When sent out a second time, his companions reported his lies and he was sent to jail.

1722 Dutchman Jacob Roggeveen managed to reach almost 65°S and reported many birds heading south towards nearby land.

1738 – 1739 Frenchman Jean-Francois-Charles Bouvet de Losier sighted Bouvet Island south of 54°.

All these early explorers had to sail 16,000 kilometres before they could even approach the 'unknown continent'. They faced fog, icebergs, 100-knot winds, damaged ships, sick crews, and enormous 18-metre rollers surging endlessly across the Southern Ocean, a place no human had ever been before them.

In 1773, Cook was on his second voyage of discovery. His aim was to explore as far south as he could. On 17 January 1773 his ships the *Resolution* and the *Adventure* became the first to cross into the Antarctic Circle. He spent several months sailing around the ice before turning north to spend the winter in New Zealand. In the summer of 1774 he headed south once more and on 30 January reached 71˚11'S, the furthest south any explorer had ever been. As he turned back, he wrote in his log that it was too dangerous to go on. He was only a day's sail from the coast of Antarctica, but pack ice and poor visibility stopped him. Four years later he made a third try to get through pack ice. He reached 77˚S, about 1770 kilometres from the South Pole and 480 kilometres south of the Antarctic Circle. He saw seal colonies on the island of South Georgia and charted the South Shetlands, South Orkneys and South Sandwich islands. He described South Georgia as a 'horrible and savage place', and thought that if there was land further south it would be cold, desolate and inhospitable.

The first sight of Antarctica

Three people, an Englishman, a Russian and an American, claimed to have been the first to sight the Antarctic mainland. An English Royal Navy officer, Edward Bransfield, sailed the *Williams* south from South Georgia and sighted the tip of Graham Land, going ashore on 30 January 1820. But the log of the *Williams* was lost, so not everyone accepts his claim as valid. Thaddeus Bellingshausen, a Russian sailor and explorer, led a Russian expedition in 1819. His two ships were the *Vostok* and the *Mirnyi*. In 1819–21 he circumnavigated Antarctica, well to the south of Captain Cook's voyages, and discovered some major pieces of land, such as Alexander Island. He reported sighting the Antarctic ice cap, but did not realise that it was the mainland. Some historians now think he saw only islands. Nathaniel Palmer, an American sealer sailing in the *Hero*, claimed to have sighted the mainland in November 1820. Non-American historians think he saw Deception Island, not a part of the mainland.

Thaddeus Bellingshausen, a Russian explorer, may have been the first to sight the Antarctic mainland in 1819–21.

Sealers make discoveries

On 7 February 1821, at 64°01'S, John Davis, an American sailing in the *Cecilia*, came ashore for an hour at what was a large body of land. It was probably Hughes Bay on the Antarctic Peninsula. James Weddell, a Scottish sealer, sailed south (74°15') into an area now known as the Weddell Sea in the *Jane* in 1822–24. He brought back the first discovered species of an inshore seal, now named after him. Even modern icebreakers have often failed to get so far south. In 1831, the British sealer James Biscoe, sailing in the *Tula*, circumnavigated Antarctica further south than ever before. He discovered Enderby Land, Adelaide and Biscoe islands. There were other British sealing voyages from 1833–39, like Peter Kemp in the *Magnet* and John Bellamy in the *Eliza Scott* and the *Sabrina*. In 1839 the first recorded woman to cross the Antarctic Circle was lost on board the *Sabrina*. Her name and nationality are not known.

Governments and scientific organisations send expeditions

France

From 1837 to 1840, Jules-Sébastien Dumont d'Urville was sent on a government expedition to find the South Magnetic Pole and explore

The two French ships, the *Astrolabe* and the *Zélée*, commanded by Dumont D'Urville hit rough seas in the Antarctic in 1838.

Antarctica. He headed south from Tierra Del Fuego for the Weddell Sea. Just below 62°S his ships *Astrolabe* and *Zélée* were trapped in pack ice for five days, before they turned towards the Antarctic Peninsula and Joinville Island. The expedition charted and mapped the northern end of Graham Land, before retreating to Chile for the winter. In 1840, the ships sailed south from Hobart, and Dumont d'Urville named Terre Adélie — and the penguin found there — after his wife. He found the approximate position of the South Magnetic Pole and reached 64°S before being driven back by severe storms.

USA

In 1840 an American naval officer, Lieutenant Charles Wilkes in the *Vincennes*, discovered Wilkes Land and charted 2400 kilometres of Antarctic coastline. He established that Antarctica was a continental land mass and not just floating ice.

Britain

In 1841–43 Lieutenant James Clark Ross, in the HMS *Erebus* and the HMS *Terror*, carried out important magnetic surveys as well as discovering the Ross Sea and Victoria Land region. James Clark Ross had been the first to reach the North Magnetic Pole in 1831 and was sent south to bag the other magnetic pole before the French or Americans got there. He headed south-east into seas where no other ships had been. When his ships hit pack ice he just kept going, as they were strongly built 'bomb' vessels strengthened to fight and survive in pack ice. After only four days the pack ice suddenly vanished and Ross sailed south into an open sea.

He saw the high mountain peaks of land, some 450 kilometres south of the Antarctic Circle. Ross named the promontory Cape Adare, landed on a nearby island and claimed the region for Britain, naming it Victoria Land. He then followed the mountainous icebound coast for 580 kilometres further south, until the way was barred by the Great Ice Barrier, a solid wall of ice up to 60 metres high, running east–west, that blocked his path to the Magnetic Pole. Here he described an active volcano and a deep bay in the Ross Sea. He named them Mt Erebus and McMurdo Sound, respectively. He wintered in New Zealand, then the following summer sailed up to the Falkland Islands. In the summer of 1842–43 the

Lieutenant James Clark Ross of Britain explored extensively in 1841–43.

expedition explored the Weddell Sea, charted areas between the Antarctic Peninsula and Joinville Island, and reached the latitude of 71°30'S.

Other expeditions

Later explorers, such as the British naval officers Wyville and Thompson in the *Challenger* in 1872–76, proved that Antarctica was a continent, not a group of islands. Bismarck Strait was charted in 1873–74 by a German sealer, Dallman, in the *Grönland*. The Larsen Ice Shelf was discovered in 1892 by the Norwegian Captain Carl Larsen, and Active Sound in 1892–93 by the Scotsmen William Bruce and W. Burn Murdoch in the *Balaena* and the *Active*.

The first confirmed landing

On 24 January 1895 the Norwegian whaling ship *Antarctic*, captained by Henrik Bull, landed a party at Cape Adare in the northern Ross Sea and spent 90 minutes ashore gathering lichens. They confirmed that in summer there was ice-free water inside the pack ice.

International interest in Antarctica

In 1895 the International Geophysical Congress urged members to send scientific teams to explore Antarctica.

The first wintering over

In 1898–1900 ten men from the well-organised Southern Cross Expedition, under leadership of Carsten Borchgrevink, spent the winter in a prefabricated hut. Zoologist Nicolai Hansen died and was the first man buried there. A sledging party reached 78°50'S, the first such journey on the Ross Ice Shelf.

The second vessel to spend winter in the pack ice was the *Gauss*, in 1901–03, with a

Carsten Borchgrevink led the Southern Cross expedition, a team of ten men, the first to winter over on the Antarctic mainland.

Men from the Southern Cross Expedition, 1898–1900, loading their ship.

German Antarctic Expedition. Their aim was research, not exploration, and the ship was trapped in pack ice in the Davis Sea. The captain, Erich von Drygalski, discovered Kaiser Wilhelm II Land. Drygalski used penguins to stoke the ship's furnace when it ran out of fuel. In 1901–04 the Swede Otto Nordenskjöld in the *Antarctic* mapped parts of the peninsula and spent two winters on Snow Hill Island.

Mirages: Early nineteenth century whalers reported an island south of Macquarie Island. Later explorers searched for this Emerald Island without success. Captain Davis in the *Aurora* sailed right through the middle of its supposed location. Satellite surveying later proved that Emerald Island did not exist. It was probably a mirage caused by differences in the way light is transmitted through layers of air. Distant mountains seem close by, icebergs hang upside down in the sky, land appears as a cloud and banks of cloud look like land.

Key Points

1. Early explorers were looking for a vast southern continent called Terra Australis.
2. Captain Cook's two ships were the first recorded ships to cross into the Antarctic Circle.
3. Many early discoveries were made by sealers looking for new sealing grounds.
4. Discovering that in summer there was ice-free waters south of the pack ice, helped explorers.
5. The first definite landing on the Antarctic continent was not made until 1895.

Whalers and sealers

Fur seals are protected against the cold by their dense pelts. Unfortunately for them, Europeans found these a very attractive material for making coats and hats. There was a big demand for sealskins.

In a time before mineral oil was easily available, people needed animal oil for lighting and soap-making. Seals and whales have a thick layer of blubber to protect themselves from the cold and good profits could be made from cargoes of animal oil. Northern seals and whales were disappearing fast, so when Captain James Cook told of huge seal colonies in the south, sealers and whalers headed for the subantarctic islands.

The survivors of the sinking of the *General Grant* made their own clothes from seal skins. Here one poses after he has been rescued. In Europe, sealskin coats were very fashionable.

The sealing industry

Firms like the British Southern Whale Fishing Company, later called Enderby Brothers, sent ships into southern waters. From 1805, they established a sealing station on Enderby Island, in the Auckland Islands. The company encouraged their captains to find new areas for whaling and sealing. Many parts of Antarctica are now named after the sealers who explored the area, or the owners of their ships.

❄ The whalers once sang: 'Beyond 40 degrees South is no law; beyond 50 degrees South is no God.'

But the sealing industry was short-lived. In 1819, the sealers from America, Britain, Australia and Argentina found the fur seal colonies. The first big recorded haul was in January 1820 when an Argentinean ship killed 14,000 animals in five weeks. In the 1821–22 season, 40 boats were hunting seals. Sealers worked the beaches until all the seals were dead. An expert could kill and skin 50 seals an hour, standing knee deep in blubber and blood. Estimates of numbers killed reach 5,500,000.

In the 1823–24 season there were 90 boats. The very next year it was all over. There were not enough seals to make a voyage profitable.

By 1890, few seals were left on the islands of the Southern Ocean. In 1936, a visitor to the South Orkney Islands, once an important sealing base, found only one seal. By 1995, however, the seal population on the South Orkneys was up to 22,000. With a hundred years of protection, and possibly an increase in their main food of krill, fur seal populations have recovered strongly.

Elephant seals and penguins

Once fur seals were gone, hunters turned to blubber-bearing elephant seals. These can weigh up to three tons, with blubber 20 centimetres thick. The cows do not have as much blubber as the bulls. The average yield for bulls was 450 kilograms of blubber. The blubber was cut into small pieces and melted down in 'trying pots' made of thick cast iron. Later, steam digesters were used. The elephant seal season lasted about three months, and four weeks later the same men started on the penguins. Hundreds of thousands of penguins were killed for their oil in the early nineteenth

Sealers at work on Campbell Island in 1914–15. The seals were clubbed to death while they lay resting or sleeping on the rocks.

century. Elephant seals and penguins are now protected and their numbers have recovered.

❄ The 1972 Convention for the Conservation of Antarctic Seals gave protection for all southern seals and put an end to commercial sealing off the Antarctic.

Whaling

Humans have a long history of hunting whales. Stone Age harpoon heads, around 5000 years old, have been found. By 1850, there were few whales left in the northern hemisphere. When explorers returned from Antarctica with tales of large numbers of whales at the edge of the ice pack, the hunt was on. Until late in the 19th century, whales in the south were protected by the distance and the savage weather. But steam-powered whalers, factory ships and the invention of harpoon guns changed this.

The first whaling took place around the Antarctic Peninsula where there were several ice-free harbours for ships. Between 1927 and 1931 over 14,000 whales were killed and processed in the Ross Sea area alone. Argentina was the first country involved in commercial whaling in the Southern Ocean, keeping it up until the late 1920s. In 1912 the first factory whaling ship arrived in the South Orkneys. Between 1920 and 1930, 3500 whales were harvested.

The whaling industry was one of the reasons countries claimed parts of Antarctica. Norway and Britain took most of the catch for the first six decades of the twentieth century and continued hunting in Antarctica until the 1960s. Japan and the USSR developed their whaling industry after about 1969.

❄ 1938 was the year of doom for whales, with the greatest number of kills ever — 46,039 whales and 500,000 tons of oil.

What a whaling station was like

At Whalers Bay, the southernmost whaling station, a visitor described the smell as unbearable. Pieces of whale floated about on all sides and bodies in the process of being butchered lay alongside the boats. At South Georgia, Shackleton's second expedition was disturbed by the awful stench from the huge bloated carcass of a whale. They towed it out to sea, but it came back.

Right: In the 1920s a man cuts up a whale caught in the Ross Sea.

Below: The death of a whale in the 1940s.

Few whales left

By 1965, despite up-to-date tracking equipment, including helicopters, the South Georgia whaling fleets saw only four blue whales the whole season.

The International Whaling Commission was established in 1946. Its aims were to govern the conduct of whaling and, from 1975, to limit the catch to sustainable levels. In 1982, the members decided to stop all commercial whaling from 1985–86. But though commercial whaling has been cut back, it has not stopped completely. Japan continues to catch minke whales, supposedly for research, but the whale meat ends up on tables.

Key Points

1. With a big demand in Europe for sealskins, sealers quickly wiped out most of the seals.
2. Seals, penguins and whales were killed for their blubber, which became oil for lamps and soap.
3. Seals and penguins are now protected and their numbers are recovering. Commercial whaling is now limited, but still continues.

The heroic age of Antarctic explorers

To be first at the Pole

Many explorers dreamed of being the first man to raise their country's flag at the Pole. As the discoverer of new lands, an explorer would become famous, perhaps rich, and definitely a national hero. Explorers also wanted to find out more about the unknown, undiscovered continent, to reveal its scientific secrets. Public appeals to raise money for expeditions used both these ideas.

Scott's first expedition 1901–04

The first trip into the interior of Antarctica

In 1900, Commander Robert Falcon Scott was appointed leader of an Antarctic expedition. He had to organise one of the most ambitious scientific expeditions ever. He was 32 years old when he applied to lead it. He had no experience in polar exploration, but was very keen on adventure, possible fame and fortune, and interested in science. Strong, lean and athletic, he was used to being a leader. He was squeamish about killing animals (he tried visiting an abattoir to get over it, but it didn't work), but was very good at handling men with tact and patience. The *Discovery*, the ship built for the expedition, was powered by steam and sail. It had a strong hull, but leaked badly, did not sail well and used too much coal.

Scott followed the navy tradition of separating the officers from the men, and treating them differently. Officers were more important; they had their meals in the ship's saloon whereas the men ate on the mess deck. Scientists counted as officers and the men called them 'sir'.

Robert Falcon Scott , the first man to really penetrate the continent, was an English naval officer and torpedo expert. This statue commemorating his life stands on the banks of the Avon River in Christchurch.

- English firms donated supplies: Cadbury's gave the expedition 1590 kilograms of chocolate. Bird's, another food supplier, gave them custard powder.

Ernest Shackleton, from the British Merchant Navy, was with Scott on this expedition. Shackleton got on well with both men and officers. He persuaded Scott to kill seals for food because he had read that fresh meat prevented scurvy. On the sledge trip towards the Pole he suffered a haemorrhage of the lungs. When the relief ship arrived, he was invalided out. He gritted his teeth as he left and said to himself: 'I'll be back at the head of my own expedition!'

Inexperience

Louis Bernacchi, an Australian scientist, had been to Antarctica with Borchgrevink in 1899, but few of the other officers or men had any direct experience of the Antarctic. However, before leaving, Scott sent his men off to the dentist: they had 92 teeth extracted and 170 holes filled.

Departure

Crowds cheered and boats hooted their horns as the expedition left London in late July 1901, for Lyttelton, New Zealand. Then, with 23 sledge dogs on board, the overloaded ship left Lyttelton for the Antarctic. As enthusiastic crowds waved them off, a sailor perched on the highest mast lost his grip, fell and was killed.

After delays, they headed south into thick sea fog. They planned to winter the ship over in the most southerly McMurdo harbour they could find. Then, the next summer, sledging parties would explore. A relief ship would arrive in summer to help with transporting sledging parties and would return some of the party to New Zealand. The *Discovery* would collect the other sledging parties, explore to the west and then refit in New Zealand. They planned further exploration in the summer of 1903.

First flight over Antarctica

A gap in the Great Ice Barrier (now called the Ross Ice Shelf) allowed the ship to moor and men to land. Scott went up in a hydrogen balloon called *Eva*. Even 180 metres up, he could see very little in the misty conditions. The valve was faulty and the fabric of the balloon tore and it came down quickly. Scott was lucky to survive.

Landing on Ross Island

The men landed on a volcanic island. It was joined to the distant mountains by the vast expanse of the ice barrier. At Hut Point they put up a large hut and kennels for the dogs. Eight months of provisions were stored ashore in case the ship was forced away or crushed by ice.

Learning how to survive

Dog sleds and skis were difficult to manage and frostbite was a constant problem. At times they did dangerous things, like camping on sea ice, and they soon learned that even just a hundred metres away from the hut they could get lost in a blizzard. With no fresh fruit and vegetables, scurvy was a problem, until they began to kill penguins and seals for fresh meat.

A group went off to Cape Crozier to leave a message for the relief ship. The overland trip involved dogs, skis and sledges. They learnt to sleep with their socks or mitts close to their bodies so they did not freeze overnight, how to put tents up in the windy conditions, how to use the cookers, and how much food to take. Much of their equipment had never been tested under such severe conditions.

After four days of travel they had only covered 32 kilometres. With food running short, one group was sent back to Hut Point. Two days later, just seven kilometres from safety, this group hit whiteout conditions. Instead of putting up the tent and waiting, they carried on. The men did not have crampons and slipped on the ice cliffs; George Vince slid down to his death. His memorial is on the summit at Hut Point. Clarence Hare, a young

The first 'flight' in Antarctica in a hydrogen balloon called Eva.

British explorer Robert F. Scott's 1902 Discovery Hut, located at Hut Point Peninsula, Ross Island.

Furthest south: Shackleton, Scott and Wilson on the first trip into the interior of the Antarctic. They reached 82°11' — the furthest south any man had been.

New Zealander, also slid down the slope, ending up unconscious in soft snow that covered his body. They had almost given him up for dead when, 48 hours later, he walked back to safety. He had survived without a tent or sleeping bag and did not even have frostbite.

The main party also had problems, but returned safely.

Winter set in and the sun disappeared for four months. The hut was less than 180 metres from the ship, with a guide rope most of the way, but men still got lost between the two. Many were badly frostbitten. To help with the long, dark days, cooped up in huts and the ship, they started a magazine, *The South Polar Times*, edited by Shackleton.

First trip into the interior

Three men, Shackleton, Edward Adrian Wilson and Scott, set out in early November to explore as far south as possible. The Pole, they knew, was too far away (2380 kilometres there and back).

Crates of supplies from expeditions can still be seen today in the historic huts built by explorers.

The hut was filled with supplies. This photograph was taken in 2006.

A support team went with them for the first two weeks. On a good day they could cover 17 kilometres, but blizzards slowed them down. All three were inexperienced and the terrain proved too rough for easy skiing. The dog teams were a disappointment, probably because the dog food was not right. They hated having to butcher the weaker dogs, one by one, to feed the stronger ones. In addition, the men were very hungry. Scott used tobacco to take the edge off his hunger and when that ran out, he tried old tea leaves. They were horrid. One night they set the tent alight and had to mend the hole.

Painful snow blindness made their eyes bloodshot and inflamed. At times, two out of the three were blind and the third only had one eye working.

❄ Human eyes are quickly damaged by the intense reflections of sunlight on ice. Later explorers learned to use protective goggles or glasses.

All three shared one sleeping bag for warmth but each morning their boots were frozen. As they walked along the coastline, they saw the gleaming black and red cliffs of the mountains rising to 4200 metres and more. On New Year's Day they turned back, having reached 82° 11'S). From 5 January, the men did all the work and the dogs walked behind. Shackleton was so ill that he could not pull the sledge, but walked alongside. They arrived back on 3 February to find that the relief ship had arrived.

They were the first men into the interior. They had covered 1766 kilometres in 81 days, climbed to 6000 metres, and knew how vast and grim the polar ice cap was. They had not changed their clothes since 2 November of the previous year.

After another winter, the *Discovery* was still stuck in the ice. By 5 January 1904, they were making plans to abandon her, when the relief ship arrived. Helped by explosives, saws, manpower, and some luck, on 16 February the ship was finally freed.

Return to England

Back in England, Scott was a national hero. He wrote a book, went back to the navy, married and began to make plans for another Antarctic trip.

Key Points

1. The expedition was led by Robert Falcon Scott.
2. Their ship was the *Discovery*.
3. They were the first to fly, in a tethered balloon, in Antarctica.
4. They were the first to explore the interior of Antarctica.
5. They were very inexperienced and had to learn fast about Antarctic conditions.

Shackleton has another go

The British Antarctic Expedition 1907–09

In 1907–09 Ernest Shackleton, backed by a loan of £20 million from William Beardmore, an industrialist, and £5000 from the Australian government, set off for Antarctica. The aim was to reach the South Pole. Shackleton had learnt from his earlier expedition with Scott and this time he took woollen clothing, fur-lined sleeping bags, Siberian huskies, Manchurian ponies and even a polar car. The huskies were not a great success. They weakened and died, probably because the dog handlers were inexperienced. Man-hauling became their main means of transport.

❄ When the ship *Nimrod* called in at New Zealand, the government swore him in as Postmaster of the Antarctic and gave him a special issue of stamps — red penny New Zealand stamps overprinted in green with the words 'King Edward VII Land'.

Ernest Shackleton's main aim was to reach the South Pole.

The car was very useful for laying depots of food and fuel, until it fell down a crevasse. It was rescued, but could not cope with soft snow.

Landing on Ross Island

Shackleton had promised Scott that he would keep away from McMurdo Sound, which Scott thought was his special area. But when Shackleton got to the Bay of Whales, much of the Great Ice Barrier had broken away. The area was so changed that he felt it was too risky to set up his base there. So he put up a hut at Cape Royds on Ross Island. Here he landed his stores, ponies and motor car, and, with difficulty, got his stores across the ice. Shackleton split his men into three groups.

First ascent of Mt Erebus

One group, led by T.W.E. David, an Australian geologist, with A. Mackay and Douglas Mawson, climbed Mt Erebus in March 1908. They were the first to climb the treacherous icy slopes. They fought against bad weather all the way and were trapped in tents by blizzards for

two days. When they reached the top, 3795 metres above sea level, they found themselves looking down into a vast crater of simmering heat and steam, 275 metres deep and 800 metres wide, with steam explosions from the bottom. Though the crater is hot, snow and ice continue up to the very summit.

To the South Magnetic Pole

The same three men set off for the South Magnetic Pole in October 1908. They pulled their heavy sledge north-west along the Ross Sea Coast, then dragged it up the Drygalski Glacier onto the vast ice plateau. They carried on north-west, rising steadily until they reached the South Magnetic Pole.

Then they had the long haul back — 420 kilometres to Drygalski Glacier. To get back to base in time to be picked up by the *Nimrod*, they had to travel 21 kilometres a day. They were very weak from living on survival rations and David had developed bad snow blindness. He handed over navigation and leadership to Douglas Mawson, only 26, on his first trip to Antarctica, but already a skilled navigator and strong leader. They forced themselves on, arriving at the sea cliffs of

Below: The vast crater of Erebus is 275 metres deep. Erebus was first climbed in 1908.

T.W.E. David, Douglas Mawson and A. Mackay, the first to the South Magnetic Pole, 2240 metres above sea level, 16 January 1909, at 72°25'S, 155°16'E on the high ice plateau of Victoria Land.

Drygalski Glacier on 31 January, with only two days' food left. They hoisted a flag. The next morning they were woken by the sound of guns. To their delight, the ship had seen their signal and was heading towards them.

They had taken 122 days to travel 2028 kilometres to claim the South Magnetic Pole for the British Empire — one of the longest unsupported man-hauling sledge journeys in Antarctica.

❄ The South Magnetic Pole: The earth's molten core creates electric currents that generate a magnetic field. The North and South Magnetic Poles are the two points on the earth's surface where the lines of magnetic force are vertical. At the South Magnetic Pole the compass points straight down. But the South Magnetic Pole moves about 5 kilometres a year. When first reached, it was on land; now it is off the coast of Adélie Land.

Western Mountains

A second group of men, led by Raymond Priestly, carried out geological exploration in the Western Mountains. They went up the Ferrar Glacier looking for fossils and doing survey work. At one point, the three men were carried out to sea on a small ice floe. They had only two days' food and were surrounded by killer whales, but they got back safely.

Nearly to the Pole

The third group, led by Shackleton himself, had just one aim, to reach the South Pole. From September, they laid out depots of food and fuel along the route. On 3 November, Shackleton, Frank Wild, Jameson Adams and Eric Marshall set off with ponies, but no skis.

The Beardmore Glacier

At the point where mountains barred their way, Shackleton spotted a great glacier that appeared like a highway to the south. It was a river of ice 190 kilometres long and 65

Shackleton and his men set a new record for the furthest exploration south. Much of their journey was over unexplored country.

kilometres wide. He named it after his sponsor. He found a route over the crevasses between the barrier and the glacier and then climbed up the glacier through the crevasses to the plateau, 2000 metres above sea level.

Reaching the ice plateau

In reasonable weather, they marched 320 kilometres south across the plateau, going past Scott's 1902 record by 590 kilometres. The Manchurian ponies were shot and eaten one by one. But when one was lost down a crevasse they knew that they would be short of food for the return journey.

Turn back or die

On 9 January they were within 180 kilometres of the Pole, at 88°23'S and 162°E, but they knew they had to turn back or die of starvation. The return journey was a series of races against death. They had some lucky breaks. The relief ship had given them up for dead and left, but saw their signal and came back for them. Later, Shackleton's wife asked him how he had found the strength to turn back when he was so close. 'I thought you would rather have a live donkey than a dead lion,' he replied.

Return to England

Shackleton returned a hero, was knighted, and received medals, awards and praise. He repaid the expedition loans by lecture tours.

Key Points

1. The *Nimrod* expedition was led by Ernest Shackleton and introduced motorised transport.
2. David, Mackay and Mawson made first ascent of Mt Erebus.
3. David, Mackay and Mawson were first to reach the South Magnetic Pole.
4. Shackleton, Adams, Wild and Marshall reached the furthest point south yet at 88°23'S, 180 kilometres from the South Geographic Pole.

Scott's second

Scott planned a second trip to the Antarctic to carry out scientific research and to get to the Pole. He was not trying to race. He did not know that Amundsen had decided to get to the South Pole first. Not until Scott was on his way south did he find out what Amundsen was up to, and by then it was too late to change his plans. Scott was burdened with lots of scientific instruments, scientists, and a major research programme.

Scott had learnt from his first expedition and took much more care in choosing his equipment. He bought skis in Norway and took a ski instructor, too. He had motorised sledges, powered by petrol engines, with a looped track of links. He also had 16 Manchurian ponies. They were very useful in unloading stores from the ship but they weakened and died in the savage weather. Scott had dogs too but his men were not used to them and the dogs did not have the right food. Scott preferred man-hauling.

Laying Depots

During the winter darkness, Apsley Cherry-Garrard, Henry Bowers and Edward Wilson sledged to Cape Crozier to collect the eggs of the emperor penguin for scientific analysis. It was a horrendous journey, with very cold temperatures and frightful storms, and they nearly died.

Following their return, Scott laid depots of food and fuel on the route to the Pole. The depot-laying trip was a training run for the trip

One of the three caterpillar tractors fell through the sea ice as it was being landed from the *Terra Nova*. The other two were not reliable or strong enough to help in getting to the Pole.

expedition (1910–12)

Apsley Cherry-Garrard and a pony called Michael.

to the Pole the following summer. The biggest depot on the Ice Barrier, 209 kilometres from Hut Point, was called One Ton Depot. There, food and fuel was left to be collected on the trip back.

Off to the Pole

Scott and Shackleton were rivals, but they also helped each other. Scott used Shackleton's notes to plan his route. There would be three sections to the trip. First, across the Great Ice Barrier (now called the Ross Ice Shelf), then up the Beardmore Glacier, and finally across the vast, cold Polar Plateau.

❄ The distance between Hut Point and the Pole as a freezing crow flies is 1190 kilometres, but difficult country, crevasses and mountains make it much further.

Journey of 1280 kilometres each way

Scott started with a big support team and several sledges. Each sledge was pulled by four men, loaded with provisions, gear for navigation, fuel and stove, and skis. The ponies were taken on the first leg, killed and eaten one by one, and some of the meat buried in the ice for the return trip. Teams of men were sent back to base at various points. On the final push to the Pole and back, the sledge was pulled by five men. The five were Scott, Bowers, Taff Evans (not to be confused with Teddy Evans), Oates and Wilson.

Bowers, Wilson and Cherry-Garrard setting off for Cape Crozier in winter. They had a terrible time.

Edward (or Teddy) Evans with a sledging theodolite. He was part of the plateau support party and nearly died of scurvy on the return trip. To navigate across the continent, they used magnetic compasses and measured the angle between the sun and the horizon with a theodolite, much as sailors did with sextants. Sledge meters kept count of how far they travelled each day.

At the Pole

They were very disappointed to see Amundsen's black flag and a campsite at the Pole. There was a note from Amundsen to Scott wishing him a safe return. Scott wrote in his diary: 'This is an awful place and terrible enough for us to have laboured to it without the reward of priority.' But Scott said nothing bitter about Amundsen; he admired what the Norwegians had accomplished.

The return journey

They had a terrible journey back. Coming down the Beardmore Glacier was very difficult and they lost their way several times. Two of the group became very ill. All five had lost too much weight and too much fat. The winter blizzards had begun and they felt the cold intensely. This, combined with their slow pace, was putting them in danger.

Terrible weather and not enough food

The weather was awful; in fact it was the worst it had been at that time of year for several years. Scott had delayed his start for the Pole until conditions were suitable for the ponies. This meant that on the return trip he hit the first of the savage winter storms. They found the caches, but there was less food and fuel than they needed in their weakened state. The caches had not been reprovisioned by the dog teams from the base as Scott had hoped. The others had last seen Scott and his party going very strongly for the Pole and did not realise that he was in trouble.

Death on the ice

Evans died first. A severe cut on his hand festered and turned bad. He may have hit his head when he fell down two crevasses. We know now that the biggest man would be most at risk from loss of weight. As a result, he got weaker and weaker, and died on the glacier.

Oates meanwhile, was having bad trouble with his feet. His toes turned black with frostbite, and an old injury to one of his legs began playing up. It was taking him one hour to get his boots on in the morning. He did not want to slow the others down any more, so decided to go out into the blizzard alone, to die. The remaining three, Scott, Wilson and Bowers, went on for one or two days but were pinned in the tent by blizzards. With no food or fuel, they were weakening rapidly and knew that they were dying. They were 20 kilometres from the main cache of One Ton Depot where food and fuel had been left for them.

Apsley Cherry-Garrard was waiting at One Ton Depot with a dog team three days before they were in the area. If he had known where they were, he could possibly have saved them. But there was no radio or any means of communication.

Five disappointed men at the South Pole. Amundsen had got there first.

With the savage winter descending, it was eight months before a party from Hut Point could set out to look for them. The search party caught sight of the tip of their death tent buried in the snow.

Henry Bowers was a sturdy, small, energetic man with red bristly hair. Nicknamed 'Birdie' because of his beaky nose, Bowers was an exceptional navigator and organiser. The photos he took lay beside his dead body for eight months. Lawrence Oates came from a privileged background of land-owning gentry and had the nickname of Titus. He helped with money for the expedition. He wrote letters home to his doting mother, grumbling about Scott. He looked after the Manchurian ponies. Edgar Evans, a Welshman known as 'Taff' was from the British navy. He was big and strong, a physical education instructor. Edward Adrian Wilson, chief scientist and artist, was a close friend of Scott and had been with him on other expeditions.

The death tent

The six men searching for them looked at the frozen bodies. Gran, the Norwegian ski instructor, said: 'Captain Scott lay in the middle, half out of his sleeping bag, Bowers on his right, and Wilson on his left, but twisted round with his head and upper body up against the tent pole.' They decided that Scott must have died last, after he had written farewell notes about the bravery of his companions. Scott and his men had died from cold and starvation. Having run out of food and fuel in a blizzard, they could go no further. Their bodies were badly affected by frostbite. Scott had written to his friend James Barrie (the writer of *Peter Pan*): 'We have had four days of storm in our tent and no-where's food or fuel.' His last diary entry was made on 29 March 1912, and they probably died on 29 or 30 March.

❄ American scientists in the 1990s established that March 1912 saw abnormally cold and unrelenting temperatures on the barrier at exactly the time that Scott and his men slowed and died. For three straight weeks temperatures were 10°C below average. This has only been repeated once in the last 38 years.

With the arrival of the *Terra Nova* in New Zealand on 13 February 1913 came the news of Scott's death. His fame, and the tragic story, spread far and wide. Although he had been beaten to the Pole by Amundsen, he and his companions became symbols of national pride and bravery.

❄ Was Scott a hero or a bungler? In the 1970s people took a new look at Captain Scott. Writers criticised his leadership, his personality, his ability as an explorer, the decisions he made and the rivalry with Shackleton. But this interpretation tended to ignore the scientific work of the Scott expedition. Since then, a biography of Scott by another polar explorer and man-

Robert Falcon Scott in his private den, Antarctica 1911.

hauler, Ranulph Fiennes, has given a more balanced view of Scott.

Scott's achievement

Amundsen got to the Pole first, but Scott had not planned it as a race. He was drawn into it by circumstances. His expedition achieved a hugely valuable survey and science programme that was less glamorous, but more useful. The route that Scott and his party chose was 97 kilometres further than Amundsen's, including 190 kilometres further on the high plateau where they struck very bad weather on the return journey. It is not surprising that the South Pole Base is named after both Amundsen and Scott.

Key Points

1. The *Terra Nova* Expedition 1910–12 was led by Robert Falcon Scott.
2. They implemented a programme of scientific research, as well as getting to the Pole.
3. When they got to the Pole, they found the Norwegian flag flying.
4. Scott and his four companions died from starvation and cold on the return trip.
5. There is some debate about Scott's leadership. Was he a hero or not?

Roald Amundsen

Norwegian explorer and first to the South Pole – Roald Amundsen.

The Norwegian explorer Roald Amundsen had been the first man to navigate the north-west passage through the Arctic. He wanted to be first to the North Pole. He borrowed the ship *Fram* for this expedition, then, in 1909, heard that Robert Peary had got there ahead of him. He decided secretly that he would be first to the South Pole instead.

The Norwegian Antarctic Expedition 1910–12

Amundsen's idea was to fool his sponsors, the general public and his English rivals, into thinking that he was interested in the Arctic, not the Antarctic. He would tell them at the last minute, so that they would not have the chance to gear themselves up for a real race. His plan worked. To keep the secret, he refused to meet Scott when Scott tried to visit him in Norway. He ordered 50 Greenland dogs and told no one but his brother, well aware that his sponsorship was for the North Pole and would be forfeit if he announced a change of plan.

Risky Approach

Amundsen took more chances than Scott. To start nearer the Pole he camped on dangerous sea ice in the Bay of Whales, started off earlier in the season, and gambled on finding a glacier up to the plateau.

- The Bay of Whales was a broad cove on the edge of the Ross Ice Shelf, formed by ice breaking away from the shelf. It disappeared in the 1950s when more of the shelf broke away.

Experienced

Amundsen and his men were confident in snow and ice. Amundsen himself had been part of the 1897–99 Belgian Antarctic expedition and was among those who made the first ever Antarctic sledging journey. He was described as 'the biggest, strongest and bravest of the crew'. His men were some of the world's best dog-sledgers and skiers.

The *Fram* lands the dogs on the ice shelf in the Bay of Whales.

Revealing the truth

As Scott's expedition in the *Terra Nova* left Cape Town for Australia and New Zealand, Amundsen set off for the south, sending Scott a telegram to be received in Melbourne: 'Beg leave to inform you *Fram* proceeding Antarctic.'

Amundsen took a tightly knit group of 19 men (far fewer than the 65 on Scott's expedition), but did not tell them about the change of plan until the boat had left the island of Madeira. They all backed the change. On board they carried with them 97 dogs, four pigs, six pigeons and a canary.

Arriving at the Bay of Whales

The *Fram* arrived on 14 January 1911 and Amundsen built a hut, which he called Framheim, on the sea ice. By wintering over on the Ross Ice Shelf he was 111 kilometres nearer the Pole. Scott's ship the *Terra Nova*, visited, and afterwards all the Norwegians caught colds. Before winter set in they set up a chain of supply depots to 80°S and marked the route with bamboo poles and flags. During the winter, the men prepared provisions and improved their tents.

Setting out for the Pole

When they made the first attempt to get to the Pole, conditions were too cold for the dogs and Amundsen had to turn back. But on 19

Improvised sounding tackle was used to work out the depth of ice.

October, Amundsen, Helmer Julius Hanssen, Olaf Bjaaland, Oscar Wisting and Helge Hassei set off for the Pole with four sledges drawn by 13 dogs each. They were all skilled skiers and experienced Arctic travellers.

❄ Olaf Bjaaland was the 1902 Nordic Ice Champion and also a skilled carpenter. Over the winter he had made the sledges lighter and faster. At the Pole, he surprised the others by producing a case of cigars to go with their seal meat dinner.

The dogs were killed as they went, to feed the men and the remaining dogs. Every day they built a beacon to mark their progress and left a record with the distance and bearings to the next destination. After climbing the Queen Maud Range of mountains (named by Amundsen) they shot 24 dogs to use as fresh meat. They called this Butcher Shop Camp. As Amundsen said: 'Twenty-four of our brave companions and faithful helpers were marked for death.' Each man had to shoot his own dogs.

The Norwegians were expert skiers and dog sledders.

In territory where no man had been before

When they reached the latitude of Shackleton's furthest south, 88°23'S, they struck out the Norwegian flag and put it on the front sledge. They laid their last depot at this spot.

❄ Amundsen admired Shackleton and said that Shackleton and his gallant companions would have their names written in stories of Antarctic exploration 'in letters of fire'.

First to the Pole

Amundsen reached the Pole on 14 December 1911, with his four companions and 52 dogs. They planted the Norwegian flag, camped and the next day circled 22 kilometres around the Pole. Amundsen left his black tent, called Poleheim, a note for Scott and a letter for King Haakon VII of Norway, for Scott to deliver should Amundsen's party not survive the return journey. They had a smooth trip back in mostly good weather, travelling between 15 and 17 kilometres a day. They returned to Framheim on 25 January with 11 dogs. They had taken 99 days and had covered 2594 kilometres. From Framheim they set off in the *Fram* to Hobart, from where Amundsen sent a cable around the world with the news.

Amundsen's achievement

It was a bold and very well organised expedition, planned specifically as a race. He did not burden himself with scientific aims and survey techniques. Unlike Scott or Shackleton, he left no maps or route sketches, though he himself used Shackleton's records. Amundsen later said: 'Our object was to reach the Pole, everything else was secondary.' A New Zealand team trying to scale the Axel

Above: First to the South Pole. Amundsen and his men set up their black tent called Poleheim.

Left: Roald Amundsen takes a sighting at the South Pole, December 1911.

Heiberg Glacier years later had to start from scratch to find the route.

Amundsen took chances, but his risks paid off. To camp on the ice was risky, but it meant that he started that much closer to the Pole. In addition, he found the Axel Heiberg Glacier, which led him onto the plateau. Amundsen died in 1928 on an air rescue mission for a crashed Arctic balloonist.

Key Points

1. Amundsen kept his plans secret until the last minute.
2. His expedition was planned as a race and was very well organised.
3. He took a small team of expert skiers and Arctic travellers.
4. He took calculated risks, but also had luck on his side — good weather and a good glacier route into the interior.
5. He was the first man to the South Pole.

Douglas Mawson's incredible journey (1911–14)

Left: A radio operator establishes contact with Australia in 1912.

Douglas Mawson, born in England, grew up in Australia and trained as a geologist. He was one of the first to carry out scientific exploration in Antarctica. This is the story of one of his survey expeditions and one of the greatest survival stories ever.

Below: Australia's claim to nearly 40 per cent of the Antarctic is based largely on Mawson's discoveries.

The 1911–14 Australasian expedition

Mawson was already an experienced Antarctic explorer, an important member of Shackleton's 1907–09 expedition. In 1911, he led an expedition to explore the continent between Cape Adare and Gaussberg. This was the 3200 kilometres of Antarctic coast lying due south of Australia. The expedition's ship, the *Aurora*, was loaded up in Hobart with supplies, dogs and scientific equipment. On the way south, six men were landed on Macquarie Island to set up a radio relay station — known as a 'wireless telegraph' in those days — to establish radio contact between Australia and Antarctica.

Cape Denison Base

The expedition set up their base in Adélie Land at Cape Denison, where they built a large hut and another wireless telegraph station — the first in Antarctica. It was a very windy spot. The climate seemed to be one long blizzard all year round. The expedition set up a number of supply depots and storm shelters for sledging parties to use the next summer. One

The hut at Cape Denison built by the Australasian Antarctic Expedition, 1911–14.

storm shelter was called 'Aladdin's cave'. It was a cavern excavated from the ice, eight kilometres inland from Cape Denison. Its entry was a vertical shaft and it had walls of pure ice, while shelves for the primus and stores were chipped out of the ice.

Dr Xavier Mertz emerging from Aladdin's Cave, a storm shelter cut from the ice, eight kilometres inland from Cape Denison.

The Western Sledging Party

Meanwhile, the *Aurora* had dropped a group, led by Frank Wild, further west. With the ship running out of coal and the men having problems finding a good place to build their hut, they had to settle on the Shackleton Ice Shelf. From this base, they were to make sledging trips around the coast, charting and exploring about 650 kilometres of coast. The ship returned to Hobart, and was expected to return to collect them all at the end of the next summer. Other groups at Cape Denison also went off sledging to explore and chart the surrounding areas.

The expedition ship *Aurora* with the men from the landing parties.

Douglas Mawson sets off

On 9 November, Mawson set off with Lieutenant Belgrave Ninnis and Dr Xavier Mertz to explore the ice plateau to the east towards Cape Adare, the western headland of the Ross Sea. Food and equipment were packed on three sledges each weighing 770 kilograms. Seventeen dogs hauled the sledges. Four weeks later they reached a point 480 kilometres from the main base. But disaster struck on 14 December.

Ninnis falls down a crevasse

Mertz was leading, followed by Mawson, and Ninnis was in the rear on the sledge with the best dogs and most of the food and fuel. Mawson heard Mertz shout out a warning about a crevasse. He looked around after a few minutes, but Ninnis was not there. Ninnis and his dog team had disappeared completely. Mawson and Mertz peered down into a gaping hole 4 metres across but saw only a dying dog and a bag of food quite out of reach. Below were the black depths of a mighty crevasse. For three hours they called and called but Ninnis was never seen again. Still in a state of shock, Mawson read out the burial service.

The two survivors were about 506 kilometres from their Cape Denison base, desperately short of food and fuel. 'May God help us,' wrote Mawson in his diary. Mawson later thought that the snow bridge across the crevasse had supported him because he was sitting on his sledge, his weight widely distributed. Ninnis, walking next to his sledge, had all his weight bearing on his foot and smashed through the arch of the thin snow bridge.

The return journey

They set out to go back, killing the remaining dogs for food. On 17 December, the last of the dogs died in its harness from starvation. They cut the tough stringy meat into small pieces and boiled it up with biscuits and raisins. Mertz was getting very sick. Both Douglas Mawson and Xavier Mertz began losing large amounts of skin. They did not know what was causing this and the other unpleasant symptoms they were experiencing.

We know now that they had Vitamin A poisoning from eating dogs' livers.

Mertz became weaker and weaker, and finally died on 7 January. Douglas Mawson lay in his makeshift tent (the main one was at the bottom of the crevasse with Ninnis) next to the dead body of Mertz and wondered how he was going to survive. He trekked the final 160 kilometres alone and with little food, using a sail on his sledge for some of the time. He survived a serious fall down a crevasse and weathered a blizzard. 'My physical condition was such that I might collapse at any moment,' he wrote. 'It was easy to sleep on in the bag and the weather outside was cruel.'

Mawson's luck changes

Then, when he had only two pounds of food left, with his hair coming out in tufts and having to bandage the hard skin of his feet back in place, he suddenly saw a strange shape looming up ahead in a snow drift. It was a cairn made of blocks of snow, with a bag of food on top and instructions detailing the route to Aladdin's cave, 37 kilometres away. It had been left by the search party. If he had been a few hundred metres on either side of the cairn, he would have missed it. Even so, in blizzard conditions and at one stage crawling on hands and knees, it took him several days to get there. But in Aladdin's cave he found fresh fruit, a sign that the supply ship had come. A blizzard raged for the next seven days, but he had food and shelter.

Return to Cape Denison hut

When the wind dropped to 50 kilometres per hour he was able to stagger on until he could see the hut. The six men left behind to search could hardly recognise him. He was half his normal weight, had lost all his hair and his face was ravaged with suffering and frostbite.

When he arrived at Cape Denison on 8 February, he could see the expedition ship *Aurora* leaving. With the men of the search party he spent another winter in the Antarctic before being picked up the next spring. Though it took him months to regain his health, the Australasian Expedition had made great advances in geographic knowledge of Antarctica and had completed an ambitious scientific programme.

Douglas Mawson went on to become Professor of Geology at Adelaide University, made two more research voyages to Antarctica, and became Sir Douglas Mawson for his work on Antarctica.

Key Points

1. Douglas Mawson led the Australasian Expedition of 1911–14, in the ship *Aurora*.
2. They set up the first radio contact between Antarctica and the rest of the world.
3. The expedition made great advances in the scientific exploration of Antarctica.
4. Mawson's survival story showed his great stamina and bravery.

Shackleton's epic journey

In 1914–17 Sir Ernest Henry Shackleton had plans to be the first to cross Antarctica from the Weddell Sea via the South Pole to McMurdo Sound. The *Endurance* left England in August 1914 with 28 men, reaching the Weddell Sea in December. Meanwhile a ten-man team in the *Aurora* headed for Cape Evans, in the Ross Sea, to lay food and fuel depots for the trans-Antarctic party. But even before he reached his starting point, Shackleton's expedition was in trouble.

The Trans-Antarctic expedition 1914–17

The *Endurance* was caught in pack ice by 15 January 1915. The ship then drifted with the ice pack away from the Antarctic shore. When the temperature fell below -50°C in February, the pack ice froze solid around the ship. They were never able to free her or navigate her again and Shackleton realised that his hopes of crossing the Antarctic continent were doomed.

During the winter, as they drifted further from the Antarctic shore, the *Endurance* was slowly being crushed by the ice. On 27 October they had to abandon the ship and set up camp on the ice. Supplies, three lifeboats, and the photographer's plates were rescued from the ship. The *Endurance* sank on 21 November. She had drifted with the pack ice for 2410 kilometres in a zigzag course.

On board the *Endurance* were Canadian huskies. During the winter on board the frozen ship, they were exercised on the sea ice. Once the ship had to be abandoned they had to be shot to save food. In addition, Mrs Chippy, the ship's cat, which belonged to the carpenter, Harry McNish, had to be shot when the ship sank. McNish shed a bitter tear and never quite forgave Shackleton.

The *Endurance* is smashed to pieces by the pack ice. The dogs look depressed. Later, they were shot.

Living on the ice floes. Frank Hurley, the photographer, and Shackleton, alongside the stove they built. It burned seal blubber for fuel.

Camping on the ice

Shackleton's men lived on the ice floes for five months, slowly drifting north. They tried to tow the boats on sledges over the ice to open water, but failed. They were forced to return to their camp, which they called Patience Camp, near the ship.

They often had to change ice floes when they broke up or got slushy. Killer whales smashed through thin ice looking for seals and penguins. Their evil little eyes peered over the edge of the ice. One man on skis was chased by a leopard seal, which dived under him, coming up ahead to cut him off from the others. He saved himself by making off at a right angle. Frank Wild shot the leopard seal, cutting it up for food. Luckily, they also found penguins to eat. The fresh meat saved them from scurvy. Occasionally, a group got cut off on another ice floe and had to be rescued.

They take to the boats

By 9 April, with the ice breaking up around them, they boarded three lifeboats. The small boats were rowed through the floes and the men camped each night on the ice.

They lived on the floating ice, drifting slowly north for five months.

One night they woke up suddenly. The ice floe had broken in half and one tent was tearing in two as a widening crack opened up right through its middle. Shackleton looked down into the crack and saw a man in the water still in his sleeping bag. With one huge effort, Shackleton grabbed him and swung him back up onto the ice. A second later, the floe came together again with a terrific thud. The saved man felt into his sleeping bag and muttered, 'Lost my bloody tin of tobacco.' One of the others said, 'You could have thanked Sir Ernest for saving you.' 'Yes,' said the dripping sailor, 'but thanking him won't bring back my tobacco.'

To Elephant Island

The boats, now named the *Stancomb-Wills,* the *Dudley Docker* and the *James Caird*, moved out into the open sea. For five days they sailed through freezing seas. The thirsty men chewed on seal meat for the moisture to be had from the blood. On 14 April they sighted Elephant Island, a gigantic mass of rock covered with a vast ice sheet. A gale separated the boats, but the next day all three landed on a rocky beach backed by a 300 metre cliff. They soon realised that the beach would be underwater with every storm and so, two days later, they made camp on a spit of land safe from the sea but very windy and exposed. With screeching winds, driving storms and the loud boom of huge chunks of ice calving off glaciers, it was a cold and miserable camp. The men lived under the *Dudley Docker*, weighing it down with rocks so that it wouldn't blow away. They cooked with blubber, their diet being seal or penguin meat and limpets stewed with seaweed.

Cut off from the world

There was not enough food to last the winter and they knew that no-one would think of looking for them on Elephant Island. Faced with the chance of a slow death from starvation and little chance of rescue, Shackleton decided to take a boat and go for help. Their best hope was South Georgia, a whaling colony, but it was 1483 kilometres away, across one of the world's most treacherous seas.

Shackleton called for volunteers. 'I am afraid it is a forlorn hope,' he said. They all volunteered. Five were chosen: Tom Crean, Timothy McCarthy, Harry McNish, John Vincent, Frank Worsley and Shackleton himself. Frank Wild was left in charge of the camp on Elephant Island.

Voyage to South Georgia

They had to cross one of the wildest, stormiest seas in the world during winter. The biggest boat, the *James Caird*, was double ended, springy and buoyant, but only seven metres long with a 1.8 metre beam. It had two masts and three sails. The boat was strengthened using wood from the other boats and a new covered deck, made from scraps of wood, boxes and their lids with pieces of old canvas sewed together, was nailed on top. Bags of shingle ballast were loaded on board, as well as food and water for 30 days. Their reindeer-skin sleeping bags were put in the bow.

With no baths or changes of clothing for six months, their suits of heavy woollen underwear, cloth trousers and heavy wool sweaters must have smelt. They also had Norwegian reindeer boots reaching nearly up to the knee, wool mittens with dogskin covers and woollen Balaclava helmets. Over all this was a suit of loose, windproof (but not waterproof) overalls and helmet.

Their food was hoosh. This was a dark brown brick, made of beef, lard, oatmeal, sugar and salt that could be made into a thick soup. They also had a small block of very sweet nut food and hot milk every four hours at night. To cook, they had to jam the primus between their feet. One man held the pot while the lumps of ice melted, then the hoosh was added.

Frank Worsley, a New Zealander, was an expert navigator and each day at noon he set

Shackleton's expedition from shipwreck to safety.

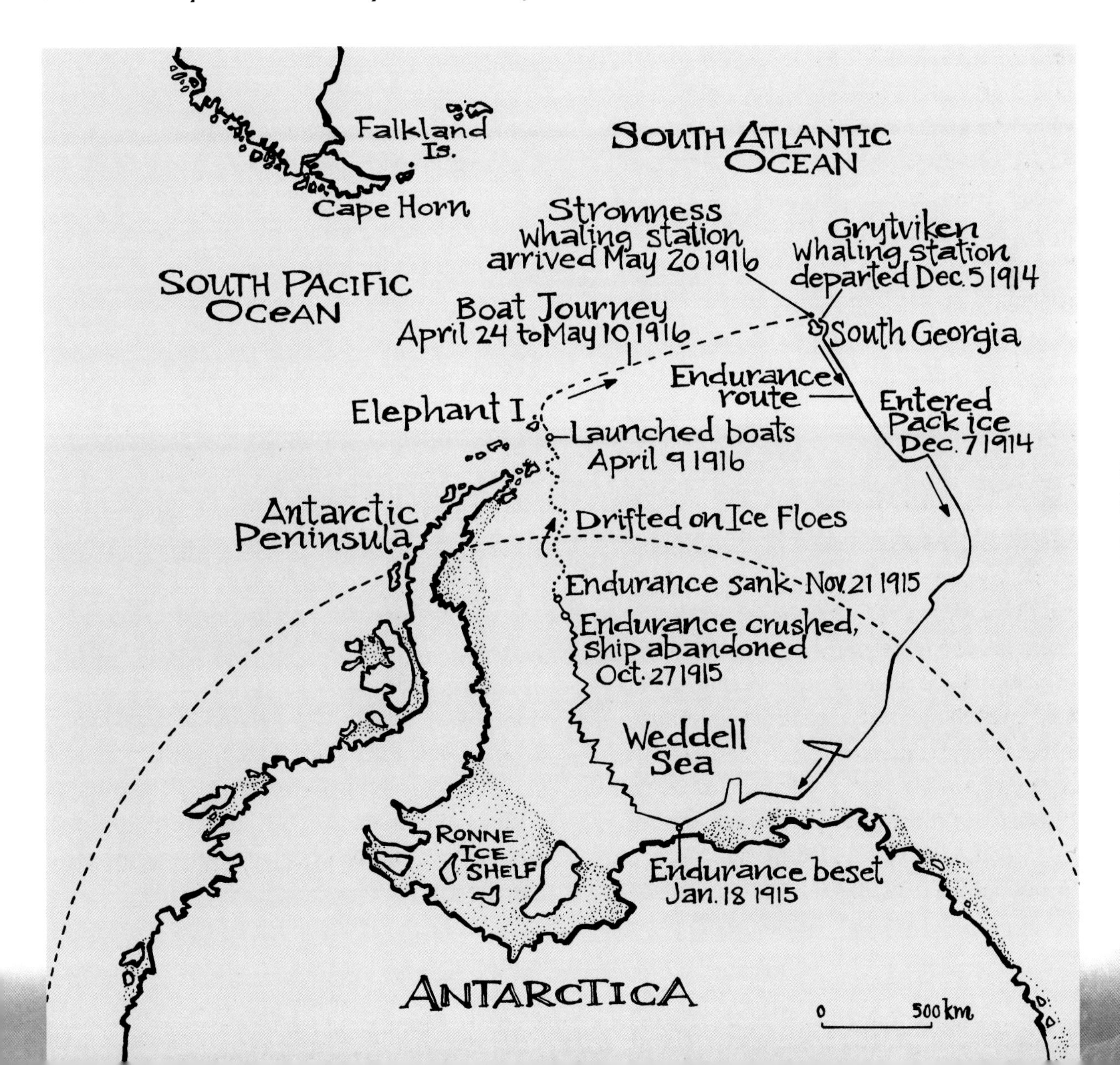

The *James Caird* was strengthened for its harrowing trip to South Georgia.

their course for Georgia. It took 16 days to get there. They had to pump water out of the boat night and day. Ice, so heavy that it threatened to sink the small boat, had to be scraped off the deck.

They were all wet through and very cramped, and the seas were mountainous. Several gales hit them with huge breaking waves. At one point Shackleton, who was on the tiller, saw the sky lightening and thought that the weather was clearing. Then he realised that what he was seeing was, in fact, an enormous wave, probably from a huge iceberg capsizing. Shackleton barely had time to shout, 'Hang on for your life,' before the boat was nearly swamped.

South Georgia at last

By the time they finally reached South Georgia, two of the men were very close to death. They were desperately thirsty, with swollen tongues. Landing on a rocky shore in screaming winds and heavy seas was very difficult, but they finally managed to beach the boat in a small cove with a tiny stream that trickled only a little brackish water — but it tasted like nectar to them. They rested in a cave, but lacked the strength to pull the boat up onto shore, as a consequence of which she bumped about all night, losing the rudder. Next morning, they pulled her up the beach and, after raiding an albatross's nest, made a 'super chicken broth'.

❄ During the night while asleep in the cave, Shackleton suddenly sat up shouting: 'Look out! Look out boys and hang on! It will get us!' He was dreaming of the big wave.

Over the next six days, ice kept them in the cove, but the rudder miraculously floated back and was rescued. They then sailed up to the head of the Sound, turning the boat upside down for shelter amid the sea elephants. They called it Peggoty Camp. They were on the opposite side of the mountainous island from the whaling settlement.

Over the mountains

On Friday 19 May 1916, at 3 a.m., three members of the party, Shackleton, Worsley and Crean, set off over the mountains for the whaling settlement. McNish had fixed 5-centimetre brass screws to their boots' soles, eight in each foot, to grip on the ice and rocks. They had three days' food, a primus, an adze, a small bowl to cook in, a spoon each, compasses, an alpine rope, chronometer and alpenstocks. Ahead were five high, rocky peaks that they had to find a way through. In misty weather, roped together, they tramped on, knee deep in the snow. They made many mistakes in their path, often having to backtrack up the mountains. At one point they deliberately slid thousands of feet down the mountain, sitting on the coiled up alpine rope, to get away from the icy cold before they froze to death. They walked all day and all night. At 7 a.m., still high in the mountains, they heard the whistle of the whaling station at Stromness Bay calling the men to work. It was the first sign

Frank Hurley, the photographer, said that this was a photograph of the rescue but it was almost certainly the men farewelling the *James Caird* as Shackleton set off to get help.

of human life they had encountered for two years. Carefully, and again using the alpine rope, they found the way down through an icy waterfall. At 3 p.m. on 20 May they came to a large shed. They had crossed the 27 kilometres of South Georgia's icy mountains in 36 hours, the first men to make the crossing.

Stumbling and tumbling — 'The fact of the matter was that our legs were a bit tired,' said Worsley — they saw two boys, who took one look at them and ran for their lives.

The Norwegian whalers were amazed by their story and welcomed them in. Later, after hot baths, and clean clothes, they began to plan the rescue of their mates.

Frank Worsley went with the whalers to collect the three men left under the upturned boat. When he arrived, the three men grumbled that 'one of our own should have come with you'. They had lived side by side with Frank every day for two years, but did not recognise him clean and shaved. The whalers also insisted on bringing back the *James Caird*, and it is now on display at Shackleton's old school in England.

Rescue from Elephant Island

Shackleton and Worsley were turned back three times by pack ice as they tried to get to Elephant Island to rescue the men left there. They worried that the castaways would die from starvation. But the fourth time they tried, they had a lucky break. There was a gap in the pack ice and the Chilean tug boat *Yelco*, skippered by Frank Worsley, was able to get to Elephant Island. It was 30 August, four months and six days since the *James Caird* had set off. Shackleton was thrilled to find that they were all alive and he whipped them off straight away, frightened that the pack ice would close in.

The Ross Sea party

Meanwhile, the Ross Sea party was also in trouble. Before all the stores were landed the *Aurora* was dragged from her moorings in a huge storm. Heavy mooring cables snapped as if they were threads and as the ship dragged out to sea, the rudder ripped off. She drifted north in the ice, then, without enough coal to get back to Antarctica, went

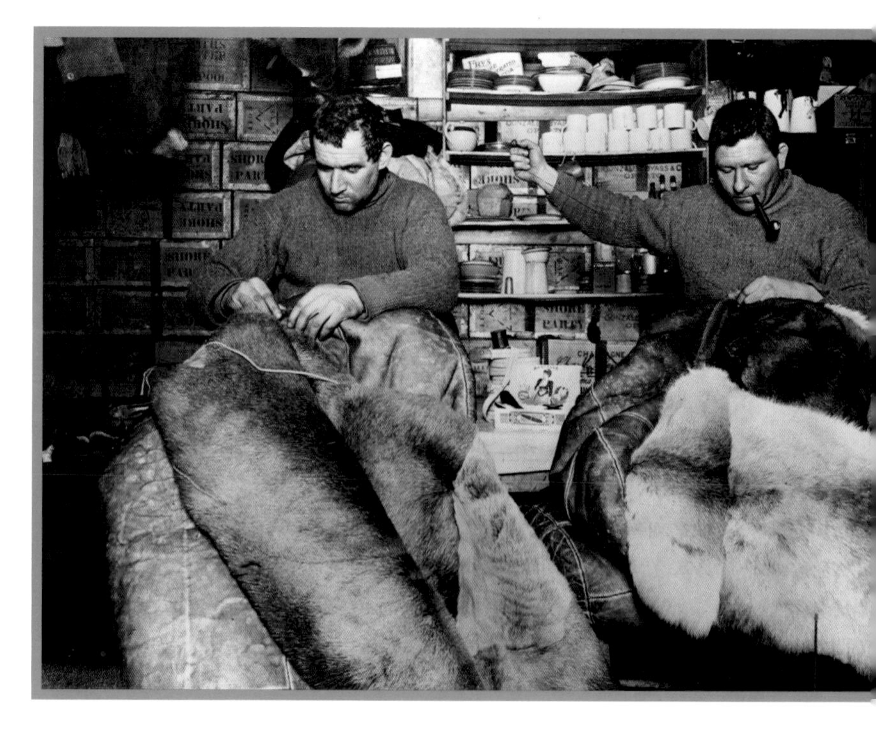

Thomas Crean with his mate Taff Evans mending sleeping bags on Scott's last expedition. Taff Evans died returning to the pole with Scott.

back to Port Chalmers in New Zealand. Ten men were stranded on shore, and they were short of supplies.

In December 1916, Shackleton and Captain Davis took the *Aurora* back to McMurdo Sound to rescue the men who had been there since 6 May 1915. They had laid depots across the Barrier to the Beardmore, covering 2872 kilometres. But when the relief ship finally arrived, three men were missing. One had died of scurvy on the barrier, and Aeneas Mackintosh (the leader) and Vincent Hayward were lost while crossing the Ross Sea Ice during a blizzard. The search party had found their tracks and then a great stretch of open water as far as the eye could reach. Their bodies were never found.

❄ In 1921–22 Sir Ernest Shackleton and Frank Wild set out again, this time to circumnavigate Antarctica. But it was to be Shackleton's final voyage. He died from a massive heart attack on board the *Quest*, while anchored in South Georgia, where he is now buried.

Personalities

For 22 years of his life, **Ernest Shackleton** had explored Antarctica. It had brought him fame and a knighthood. He had forced his way to within 156 kilometres of the Pole and had returned with all his men. Many discoveries, such as the Beardmore Glacier, and 320 kilometres of coastline, had been added to the map. A group under his command had climbed Erebus and reached the South Magnetic Pole. He had conquered scurvy and never lost a man under his immediate protection. Some have criticised his plan to cross the Antarctic in 1914, but all agree that he always led from the front and cared for his men's health and mental stamina. He was certainly respected and admired by his men.

Thomas Crean ran away from home at the age of 15 to join the navy, after a row with his father over who had let the cows into the potato paddock. In 1901, he joined Scott's first expedition to Antarctica. Scott was impressed by the tall, powerfully built Irish sailor who could always be trusted to obey orders. Tom Crean was strong and fearless. He returned to Antarctica with Scott's 1910–13 second expedition. A member of the plateau support party, he had a tough time returning to base. Teddy Evans, the leader of the three-man group, was dying of scurvy. When the other two could tow him no further on their sledge, Crean set off for help. Despite being worn out by three and a half months of hard trekking, he walked alone for 56 kilometres, with no tent and with only a few biscuits and two pieces of chocolate. It took him 18 hours, without stopping, through

Frank Wild came from the British navy and was an experienced Antarctic explorer. He was with Shackleton when they tried to reach the Pole. He wintered over on the Shackleton Ice Shelf 1911–14 with the Australasian Expedition and was Shackleton's second in command during the 1914–17 expedition. Left in charge of the camp on Elephant Island, he kept morale high in terrible conditions, organised a hut from two boats and scraps of old tents, and was scrupulously fair in everything. Throughout the ordeal he remained respected and popular. Every day he would say 'Roll up your bags boys, the Boss may be coming today' — even though he had, privately, given up hope of rescue.

dangerous crevasses and strong winds, to finally reach Hut Point and a rescue party.

With Shackleton in 1914–17, he sailed to South Georgia singing a cheerful, tuneless song as he steered the *James Caird* through horrendous seas. He retired to run a pub in Ireland which he called the South Pole Inn. He was neither an officer nor a scientist but showed that what mattered in Antarctica was not social origins and education but mental and physical stamina. Tom Crean had plenty of both.

Frank Worsley born in England and grew up in New Zealand. He went to sea at the age of 16 and joined the British navy. He was the captain of the *Endurance*. His brilliant navigation after the loss of the *Endurance* is widely credited as having saved Shackleton's men.

Harry McNish, the ship's carpenter, worked hard on preparing the small boats for the open sea. He could be a bit prickly and difficult. Shackleton did not nominate him for a Polar Medal even though he shared the hardships of the voyage to South Georgia. Later, he lived in New Zealand, and is buried in the Karori Cemetery in Wellington. The New Zealand Antarctic Society arranged for a statue of Mrs Chippy to mark his grave.

Key Points

1. In 1914, Shackleton planned to cross the Antarctic from the Weddell Sea area, through the Pole to McMurdo Sound.
2. His plan came unstuck when the *Endurance* froze solid in pack ice.
3. After the ship sank, his men lived for five months on floating ice, then reached Elephant Island.
4. Shackleton and five others made a brave voyage across 1483 kilometres of the wild southern ocean in winter, to reach South Georgia.
5. Then Shackleton, Worsley and Crean climbed over unexplored, unmapped mountains and glaciers to reach the whaling settlement.
6. On the fourth attempt they rescued the men from Elephant Island, and later were able to rescue the men left by the *Aurora* in the Ross Sea area.

Aeroplanes, adventurers & international rivalry (1925–1957)

International rivalry

Surveying and discovering parts of Antarctica was a way of establishing a country's claim of ownership. Countries were keen to exploit Antarctica's resources, such as the whaling or fishing industry.

First powered flight

In the summer of 1928–29, Australian pilot Hubert Wilkins and the American Carl Eielson surveyed and photographed the Antarctic Peninsula in a Lockheed Vega monoplane.

Private American expeditions

Richard Evelyn Byrd took a plane to Antarctica in 1928–30, as part of a very well-equipped private expedition. In November 1929, as he and his crew claimed they were over the South Pole dropping the American flag, they radioed back to their base in Antarctica. The message was sent on and immediately broadcast by loudspeaker in Times Square, New York. On his second expedition in 1933–35, he made air

Richard Evelyn Byrd, later Admiral Byrd, with his dog Igloo in 1930.

A seaplane used in Richard Byrd's 1928–30 expedition.

surveys of over one million square kilometres. He showed that, with no strait connecting the Ross and Weddell Seas, Antarctica was a single continent.

He launched American involvement in Antarctica, organised scientific research programmes and was the first to use tractors successfully. He once spent the winter alone in a weather station measuring three paces by four paces, 198 kilometres inland, until he became ill from gas poisoning and had to be rescued. His bases were called Little America I and II.

Landing a plane on inland Antarctica

Lincoln Ellsworth, a wealthy American adventurer, flew a Northrop monoplane from the Peninsula to the Bay of Whales in 1935–36,

A seaplane used in Richard Byrd's 1928–30 expedition.

crossing the continent in three stages. He and his pilot, Herbert Hollick-Kenyon, ran out of fuel 25 kilometres short of the American Base and had to walk. They had flown 3360 kilometres. In 1938, Ellsworth returned, flying over Wilkes Land, part of Australian Antarctic Territory, to claim it for the USA.

Operation Highjump

In 1946–47, Richard Byrd, now Admiral Byrd, together with Admiral Couzen led an enormous US Navy expedition with 13 ships, including icebreakers and submarines. They carried 4700 men, and 23 aircraft and helicopters to Antarctica. It was the first large-scale use of aircraft in Antarctica. They surveyed 6,240,000 square kilometres, photographing 60% of the coastline.

The first intercontinental flights

The first explorers had to get to Antarctica by sea. In 1955–56 the US Navy made the first intercontinental flights from Christchurch to McMurdo Sound. Lan Chile made the first tourist flights over Antarctica on 22 December 1956.

Britain and Australasia

Of the British expeditions conducting research in Antarctic waters, the most extensive was BANZARE, a British–Australian–New Zealand Antarctic Research Expedition in 1929–31. Led by Douglas Mawson, the expedition fixed the boundaries of Australian Antarctic Territory. They investigated whaling, studied the geology and made weather observations.

As well as discovering and charting long stretches of coastline, they collected much scientific data.

Norwegian discoveries and activities

In 1927, an expedition managed to land on Bouvet Island. In 1929–30, with air reconnaissance, Lars Christensen made extensive discoveries in Queen Maud Land.

Women in Antarctica

A Norwegian, Mrs Mikkelson, became the first woman to set foot on the continent in1935–37. Norway, Russia and America were the first countries to involve women in their polar programmes.

War

In 1938, France and Britain negotiated the boundaries of their claims in Antarctica. As the world moved towards World War II, Antarctica was drawn into the rivalry between Germany and the Allies.

In 1938–39, the explorer Alfred Ritscher arrived in the *Schwabenland,* carrying two 10-ton Wal seaplanes on board. In March 1939, he announced that he had discovered and surveyed 216,000 square kilometres of Antarctica. Swastika markers had been dropped from the air to mark out territory. After the war, Germany did not claim this land.

American claims

In 1939–41 Richard Byrd was back with an official government expedition, to establish American claims. Scientific work and surveys were performed by the Americans. A giant snow cruiser was tried out. It contained not only living quarters and a year's supply of food and fuel, but also a small aeroplane on its roof. It was a flop. Far too heavy, it moved only five kilometres.

Lincoln Ellsworth, American aviator.

Arguments over the Antarctic Peninsula

Britain, Argentina and Chile all wanted the Antarctic Peninsula. During the war, a secret British naval expedition, called Operation Tabarin, set up research stations on the peninsula to make it clear to Argentina and Chile that the British

The Banzare Antarctice Expedition, 1929–31, with Sir Douglas Mawson, fourth from left in the middle row.

were there to stay. After the war, this became the British Antarctic Survey.

Peacetime co-operation

After World War II, more countries began to think about working together in Antarctica. In 1949–52, Norwegian John Giaever led a scientific expedition of Norwegian, British, and Swedish researchers to Queen Maud Land. This was the first fully international expedition.

Key Points

1. Aeroplanes made it possible to survey vast areas of Antarctica.
2. Antarctica was drawn into international rivalries.
3. Competition for resources led countries to claim ownership of large areas of land.
4. After the war, people started to think about working together in Antarctica.

The first International Geophysical Year (1957–58)

International scientists decided to work together for one special year to understand the earth's environment, concentrating on Antarctica. Twelve countries set up about 60 research stations, observatories and laboratories. It was hoped that making science the focus would calm the tensions over who owned what in Antarctica.

- For the first International Geophysical Year scientists chose 1957–58, when a lot of sunspot activity was expected. Improved technology could be used to study all of the earth, especially outer space and Antarctica. The earlier International Polar Years, 1882–83 and 1932–33, had been mostly concerned with the Arctic.

- Russia (then known as the USSR) built Vostok station at the Pole of Inaccessibility and another station close to the South Magnetic Pole.

- The USA called their programme Operation Deepfreeze and established five bases including McMurdo and Scott-Amundsen base at the South Pole. In October 1956, US Rear Admiral George Dufek landed an aircraft at the Pole. He was the first man there since Scott and Amundsen.

US Navy Rear Admiral George Dufek talking to New Zealand pilots in Antarctica, 1956.

- Other countries also participated in Antarctic research. Britain had 14 stations, and Argentina, Chile, France, Australia, Belgium, Japan, Norway, South Africa and New Zealand were also involved.

A US air force c-124 aircraft unloads cargo at McMurdo Station in 1956.

The work done in the IGY

Geologists, seismologists, glaciologists, oceanographers and atmospheric scientists gathered data and the first overland crossing of the continent was made. Aircraft surveyed thousands of kilometres, so that little of Antarctica remained undiscovered. At the end of that year, the US President, Dwight Eisenhower, invited the eleven other Antarctic nations to Washington for a conference that led to the signing of the Antarctic Treaty.

❄ Geologists study the structure of the earth. Seismologists study the movement of the earth, including earthquakes. Glaciologists study the action of ice.

Commonwealth Trans-Antarctic expedition 1955–58

As their part in the IGY, New Zealand, South Africa, Australia and Britain funded an expedition led by Dr Vivian Fuchs. The plan was to cross the continent using snow vehicles. They also wanted to discover the depth of the ice sheet and the form of the rock surface beneath.

Sir Edmund Hillary was keen to go. Fuchs explained to Hillary how the British party would drive their vehicles from the Weddell Sea coast, through the Pole, across the Polar Plateau and down the Ferrar Glacier to

Sir Edmund Hillary, Dr Vivian Fuchs and Rear Admiral George Dufek at the South Pole, 20 January 1958. Hillary is the one with the big grin!

McMurdo Sound. Fuchs hoped that the New Zealanders would set up a base camp on the edge of the Ross Sea and find a route up the glacier. He hoped that they would lay a food and fuel depot 400 kilometres inland on the edge of the Polar Plateau for the British crossing party. But the honour and glory of getting to the Pole overland would be for the British.

Fuchs emphasised the importance of the scientific results for the IGY 1957–58. For Hillary it sounded like a jolly neat adventure, as well.

Fuchs needed extra money from New Zealand and thought that involving Hillary would be the way to get it. He was right. In 1955, the New Zealand Government formed the Ross Sea Committee and invited Hillary to lead the New Zealand Party. Antarctic Society activities helped create public interest. Schools were able to adopt a husky and individuals could buy a 'Share in Adventure' certificate. New Zealand raised more money per capita than the UK.

Setting up Shackleton Base

First Fuchs and Hillary took a ship into the Weddell Sea in the summer of 1955–56 to establish Shackleton Base. A small party, supplies and building materials were to be landed, to winter over and prepare for the arrival of the main party. Hillary took careful note of all the problems. Unloading cargo onto the sea ice was difficult and dangerous.

Setting up Scott Base

In December 1956, Hillary set up a New Zealand base in McMurdo Sound. Having learnt from the problems they had experienced in the Weddell Sea, his preparations were very thorough. Even before they left New Zealand, his team practised getting the prefab building up quickly, using tractors on the Tasman Glacier and camping in the snow. When they arrived at Butter Point, the proposed site for the new base, it became apparent that it was unsuitable. There was no flat snow for the aircraft landings and the Ferrar Glacier had a deep tide crack between the foot of the moraine hill and the sea ice. They decided instead on Pram Point and the Scott Base building was erected quickly.

❄ Three kilometres from the American Base at McMurdo, Pram Point is where Shackleton left a pram dinghy.

Both parties, British and New Zealand, were to move to the Pole in the following spring. Fuchs had three large Sno-Cats on four track pontoons, two Weasels and a converted tractor. Hillary was going to use three modified

The US Navy gave Hillary a Weasel. It was very useful.

Left: Hillary also adapted Ferguson farm tractors.

Ferguson farm tractors and a Weasel.

Hillary and Fuchs had an uneasy relationship. Fuchs wanted New Zealand help, but under his control. Edmund Hillary was ready for adventure and bold action. The two ideas did not sit easily together. Both Fuchs and Hillary would be exploring unknown areas. They were able to use small aircraft for support, but even so, driving tractors or Sno-Cats in heavily crevassed areas would be very dangerous.

A route up to the Plateau

The New Zealanders used light aircraft to reconnoitre and fly supplies ahead. The Skelton Glacier seemed the best route. Dog teams helped establish depots, one at 290 kilometres and another at 467 kilometres from Scott Base. Tractors were used to unload supplies. To try out the tractors on a long trip, they made a test run to Cape Crozier, about 80 kilometres from Scott Base.

This was the same trip which Apsley Cherry-Garrard described in his book *The Worst Journey in the World*, when three members of Scott's party set off during the dark winter to collect emperor penguin eggs. They only just survived. The New Zealanders made it an autumn trip and in spite of very cold temperatures, it was a success. They found the old, very basic rock shelter used by Wilson, Bowers and Cherry-Garrard, a sledge and two rolls of unexposed film.

Wintering over

At the new Scott Base, they were hit by some very severe storms, some lasting a week or more. Meanwhile, they prepared for the summer science programme. Two groups of surveyors and geologists with dog teams were to make an exploration of remote areas in mountains to the west of Beardmore Glacier.

Hillary's Plans

Hillary's job was to lay more depots for the British crossing party. But he also hoped to

A Sno-cat hits its first crevasse.

Edmund Hillary, Derek Wright and Murray Ellis at the South Pole, 1958. The Weasel had to be abandoned on the way, but the tractors were still in one piece, though tired. They had travelled over 2000 kilometres of snow and ice, crevasses and sastrugi – fluted ridges carved into hard ice by the wind. They can be a few centimetres high or over a metre high.

In 1957, a winter storm tore the wings off this UC-1 Otter aircraft and hurtled the fuselage over 300 metres away.

carry on to the South Pole, though neither his bosses, the Ross Sea Committee in charge of the New Zealand effort, nor Fuchs, were keen on this idea.

The New Zealanders set off

Hillary and his party started off in mid-October. They had one Weasel and three Ferguson tractors towing fully laden sledges. The vehicles were very slow when they hit soft snow. They were even slower when they hit crevasse country. A man had to go ahead to find a safe route. Even then, it was dangerous. The three tractors were roped together. When snow bridges suddenly collapsed, a tractor would disappear down a crevasse and the other two would pull it out. With 24 hours of daylight they were able to move at night as well as day.

To the Pole

After they had laid the final depot, Hillary and his team decided push on to the Pole. They arrived there on 4 January. The British arrived on 20 January.

To Scott Base

Guided by Hillary, the expedition set out from the Pole on 24 January. For much of the way the Sno-Cats were able to follow tracks left by Hillary's tractors. They arrived at Scott Base, on 2 March, within the 100 days that Fuchs had allowed for the trip.

A successful traverse

Fuchs had crossed Antarctica. Ed Hillary's party, the first to reach the Pole overland since Scott, had changed a depot-laying chore into an ambitious and brave exploit. New Zealand survey parties explored over 103,600 square kilometres of uncharted continent.

Science as well

IGY scientists at Scott Base kept meteorological records and monitored seismic activity, geomagnetic field changes, fish levels, and tide and current changes. They had explored and carried out extensive geological research over vast unvisited areas of the continent. It was the beginning of a wide and successful research programme that is still being carried out.

Key Points

1. The International Geophysical Year, 1957–58, involved research programmes by scientists from many countries.
2. Antarctica was the special focus.
3. The emphasis on science took the heat out of international tensions about who owned what in Antarctica.
4. Scott Base was set up by New Zealand as part of our contribution to the IGY.
5. Vivian Fuchs, with Edmund Hillary's help, completed a successful crossing of Antarctica.
6. Ed Hillary's party, using farm tractors, was the first to travel overland to the Pole since Scott.

International involvement & treaties

The *Kainan Maru* landed a Japanese expedition in Antarctica in 1910–12.

Early discoveries led to arguments

The Antarctic Peninsula was O'Higgins Land to the Chileans but San Martin Land to the Argentineans. To Englishmen, it was Graham Land, but was Palmer Land to Americans.

By international agreement it is now called the Antarctic Peninsula; Graham Land is the northern half and Palmer Land the southern half.

Claims of ownership

By the first half of the twentieth century, seven nations claimed that they owned pie-shaped bits of Antarctica. Some British claims were transferred to New Zealand and Australia. Some nations explored but did not make claims.

A Japanese expedition led by Lieutenant Nobu Shirase left Tokyo in 1910 with the aim of reaching the Pole. They got as far south as 74° 16' before bad weather and heavy ice stopped them. They came back in 1912, for scientific work, establishing a base camp at the Bay of Whales. There they met the crew from the *Fram,* waiting for Amundsen to return from the Pole. A seven-man sledging team reached 80°5'S, 415 kilometres inland before turning back. Japan did not make a formal claim for land but said it had rights in Antarctica.

Claims get nasty

During World War II the nearby seas were used by Nazi raiders. In 1943, the British discovered that Argentine visitors had put up signs claiming the northern Antarctic Peninsula. They put a Union Jack there instead, and returned the brass cylinder containing the new claim to the Argentine government. The British, worried that Argentina might be on the German side in the war, set up a base on Deception Island. In the meantime, the Argentinean government took away the British flag and put up an Argentinean flag in its place. The British came back and changed the flags again. The British, Chileans and Argentineans all built stations to back up their claims to the

Stamps were issued by some countries to demonstrate their claim. For the 1907–09 British Antarctic Expedition, New Zealand issued 24,000 copies of the New Zealand 'Penny Universal' overprinted with the words ' King Edward VII Land'.

Antarctic Peninsula. The stations were close and used mostly for spying on each other. But all three nations worried about US claims, too. There was violence once in 1952, when some sailors from the Argentinean navy fired at a British weather station party.

By the mid-1950s many nations were involved in Antarctica. Some had commercial activities like whaling or fishing, some had scientific programmes or weather stations, and nearly all were pushing their rights to control specific areas.

Among the claims by the mid-1950s were: Australia, with stations on Heard and Macquarie islands, and with Mawson Station on the mainland coast of MacRobertson Land; South Africa claimed Prince Edward and Marion islands; France had permanent bases in the Kerguelen and Crozet islands and had surveyed much of the Adélie Land Coast; Argentina had established General Belgrano Station on the Filchner Ice Shelf; Norway had the Maudheim base on Queen Maud coast; and meanwhile the USA and USSR didn't recognise other nations' claims.

International Geophysical Year of 1957–58

The year was about countries and scientists working together. Science was the main focus, not who owned what. When the IGY ended, there were worries that quarrels would start again, but, under the leadership of the USA, 12 governments agreed to sort something out.

These flags at McMurdo Station are of the original 12 nations who signed the Antarctic Treaty.

An Antarctic toothfish being examined and measured by scientists.

Antarctic Treaty

After long negotiations at a conference in Washington, a treaty was signed in 1959 (1 December) by 12 countries and came into force in 1961 (June 23). Article IV was the most important. It did not try to sort out who owned what in Antarctica, but just stated that it would accept the situation that existed in 1959.

Article I: Antarctica was to be used for peace only, with no military activities of any sort.

Article II: Freedom of scientific investigation in Antarctica would continue (as in the IGY).

Article III: Countries agreed to work together, to exchange information, to exchange scientists, and to make observations freely available.

Article IV: Ownership of land — the status quo of 1959 was recognised but no new claims or bigger claims were to be made.

Article V: No nuclear explosions or disposal of radioactive waste was allowed in Antarctica, but the peaceful use of nuclear power was permitted.

Other clauses referred arguments to the International Court of Justice (none up to 2002), and allowed for the appointment of observers to inspect all stations. Exchanging scientists helped in this. The inspections are expensive and time-consuming so the USA carried out most of them. No violations had been detected by 2002. Another clause arranges for meetings to be held every year (Antarctic Treaty Consultative Meetings) and for changing the treaty if all agree.

Who signed?

Argentina, Australia, Belgium, Chile, France, Japan, New Zealand, Norway, South Africa, USSR, Britain and the USA all signed the treaty.

Other states who have performed research in Antarctica are consultative countries: Brazil, Bulgaria, China, Ecuador, Finland, Germany, India, Italy, the Netherlands, Poland, Peru, Republic of Korea, Sweden, Spain and Uruguay. By May 2000, another seventeen states had accepted the treaty without becoming consultative parties.

Protecting the environment

Improving technology meant that exploiting oil and mineral resources in Antarctica was becoming possible and countries began to consider investigating Antarctica's resources. To beef up the Antarctic Treaty, a new agreement aimed at protecting the Antarctic environment was negotiated.

Madrid Protocol

The protocol on Environmental Protection to the Antarctic Treaty was signed on 4 October 1991 in Madrid, and came into force on 14 January 1998, after all of the consultative parties to the Antarctic Treaty agreed to it.

No minerals and oil in the Antarctic were to be exploited for 50 years. Rules were set up to protect animals and plants, to dispose of waste, to prevent marine pollution, and to protect and manage the area. A full conference is to review the situation in 2041.

An environmental protection committee was set up to give advice and make recommendations. But there have been problems. Not all countries have agreed to the protocol and not all have followed the rules completely.

What do countries disagree about?

Fishing

Subantarctic islands owned by countries have economic exclusion zones. For example, Campbell Island is part of New Zealand, and Macquarie Island is part of Australia. But if ownership is not clear, there are no such zones. The biggest problem is overfishing: once this applied to seals and whales; now krill, squid and finfish such as rock cod, ice fish, mackerel and Patagonian toothfish are in jeopardy. But stopping the illegal fishing is difficult. There is trouble, too, between Japanese whaling fleets and Greenpeace activists.

War

In 1982, when Argentina invaded the Falkland Islands and South Georgia, both later recaptured by the British, there were casualties on both sides. The Antarctic itself remained a zone of peace. Even during the war, Argentinean and British diplomats were meeting to discuss marine and mineral resources.

New Zealand's position

In 1923, Britain made a claim for the Ross Dependency on behalf of New Zealand. But New Zealand has always been keen on making the Antarctic an international area, and establishing it as a world park. New Zealand took part in the IGY building Scott Base. It is a strong supporter of the Antarctic Treaty and carried out one of the first inspections of other bases under Article VII of the treaty. New Zealand has signed the Madrid Protocol. It is keen on looking after its fishing rights in the Southern Ocean and on conserving fishing stocks.

Key Points

1. Countries have wanted to claim parts of Antarctica, so that they could exploit its resources.
2. After the IGY many countries agreed to an international treaty.
3. The Antarctic Treaty meant that Antarctica was to remain a zone of peace, and claims of ownership as of 1959 were just accepted.
4. The Madrid Protocol meant that no minerals or oil were to be exploited for 50 years.
5. There are still problems regarding fishing and whaling.
6. New Zealand is a strong supporter of the Antarctic Treaty.

Humans in Antarctica today

Scientists, adventurers and tourists are the visitors to Antarctica today.

Scientists

Scientists focus on weather, climate, volcanoes, marine biology, loss of ozone, and space research. Their work includes studying how glaciers behave and taking core samples from deep within the ice sheet. Scientists check for signs that industrial pollutants have affected the environment. Some find out how fish and animals adapt to living in the cold.

❄ Over millions of years the ice has built up a frozen record of pollen, dust, volcanic ash and meteorites. These provide clues about climate and weather in the past.

❄ Ozone is a version of oxygen with three atoms per molecule (normal oxygen has two). At ground level it is a dangerous pollutant, but at altitude it blocks the passage of harmful ultraviolet light.

An example of scientific activity in Antarctica: The Andrill Programme

International scientists, including several from University of Otago, are trying to learn more about the effects of global warming by seeing how ice sheets behaved millions of years ago. In a US$30 million (NZ$43.4 million) Antarctic drilling programme, they have drilled more than 1020 metres into the seabed beneath the ice sheets. Once they have a drill core they can examine it for evidence of climate changes.

The drill site is at the Ross Ice Shelf, 12 kilometres south-east of Scott Base. The drill itself travelled through 100 metres of ice shelf and 900 metres of water to reach the sea bed. There was 2 kilometres of drill hanging off the Andrill rig in the deepest drill hole ever drilled in Antarctica. The drilling system was designed by a New Zealander from Victoria University and the drill team is from Porirua.

Private adventurers

Technological advances, such as the Nansen primus stove, icebreakers, mechanised transport, radio communications systems and aircraft have made it easier to survive in Antarctic conditions.

In the 1980s and 1990s small teams of men on skis dragging sledges behind them

Left: The Andrill camp on the Ross Ice Shelf in 2006.

Above: US scientist Jennifer Mercer watches a balloon carrying instruments to measure the amount of ozone in the atmosphere.

reached the North and South Poles and returned. A Norwegian, Borg Ousland, even travelled alone on skis across the entire Antarctic continent without any aerial support. Even with modern technology and routes mapped out by earlier explorers, these adventurers have needed tremendous endurance and courage. Towed sometimes on skis by quadrafoil parachutes driven by strong winds, they have had tiny but powerful radios to call for help if necessary. GPS navigation

The battered tail of the Air New Zealand DC-10 after the crash on Mt Erebus in 1979. 257 people were killed. After this there were no more overflights until 1994. Such flights can take 12 hours with four hours spent over Antarctica.

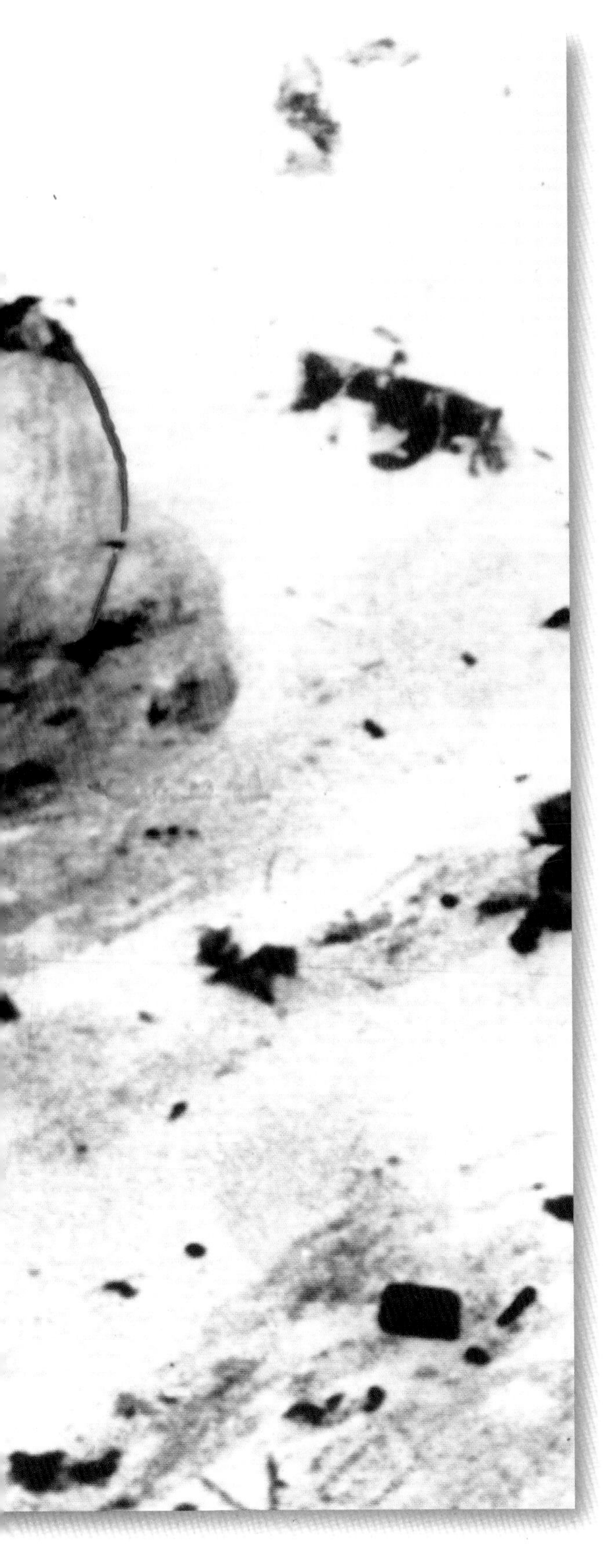

From deep under the ocean floor, this sediment core has been sliced in half so that Andrill scientists can examine it.

systems tell them precisely where they are.

Examples of adventurers include Monica Kristensen, who led dog teams to reach the South Pole by Amundsen's route but had to turn back 437 kilometres short of the Pole in 1986–87. In 1992–93, Ann Bancroft led the American Women's Expedition in which four women hauled sledges to the South Pole. They were the first women to reach the South Pole by foot. In 1993, Ranulph Fiennes and Mike Stroud made the first unsupported crossing of the Antarctic, and in 1998, Peter Hillary and two companions, Eric Philips and Jon Muir, made the first ascent up the Shackleton Glacier to the Polar Plateau and on to the Pole.

But private adventurers often have to be rescued. This is very expensive and often dangerous for the rescuers, so they are not

Towing a sledge laden with food and fuel, Eric Philips makes a test run over sea ice near Scott Base in 1998.

very popular with scientists. The dangers are great. In 1998, three people skydiving at the South Pole were killed when their parachutes failed.

Tourists began to visit in the late 1950s on cruise ships, yachts or on aircraft overflights. Ship based tourism is the most common. It is expensive to be a tourist in Antarctica, but tourism is growing. In 1999–2000 about 14,762 people travelled to Antarctica with private expeditions, mostly cruises.

People worry about the effect of tourism on the environment, about having to rescue tourists or tourist ships and scientists complain about the disruption to science programmes. Others feel it makes people more aware of the unique environment of Antarctica and the importance of science.

Tourists coming ashore at McMurdo Sound.

Key Points

1. Scientists in many different fields find the Antarctic an ideal place for research.
2. Adventurers, helped by modern technology, are also drawn to the wilderness of Antarctica.
3. Tourists, too, are increasingly drawn to the beauty, the interesting wildlife and the wilderness of Antarctica.
4. There are many arguments over whether tourists and adventurers are a good thing for Antarctica.

Epilogue — What does the future hold for Antarctica?

Giant icebergs in McMurdo Sound.

Global warming

Global warming may change Antarctica in the future. Ice sheets are already retreating, with huge icebergs calving off. In 1995, one from the Larsen Ice Sheet measured 70 kilometres long and 25 kilometres wide.

Minerals

We know that Antarctica is like Australia geologically and has great deposits of iron ore, gold, silver, platinum, uranium, copper, lead, zinc, titanium, cobalt and manganese. Will nations be able to resist exploiting these?

Future US base at the South Pole

The USA is building a new base at the South Geographic Pole. The first one was built in 1957 during the International Geophysical Year. It was replaced in 1975 by a geodesic dome 50 metres in diameter, with buildings inside. But strong winds and a build-up of snow buried it each year in winter.

Fifty years later, with many new science projects about to begin, a new high-tech home is needed. It will cost the National Science Foundation US$150 million and is likely to be completed in 2008 or 2009.

The new building, of 6000 square metres, will have the profile of an aircraft wing and will be built above the ground on a series of columns. The constant wind at the Pole will flow above and below the structure, and slow down the build-up of snow. When it does become clogged, the engineers can lift the whole building up on hydraulic jacks. Computer models indicate that it will be 15 years before the first jacking up is required. They can do this twice, giving the building a 40–50 year lifetime. Flexible materials used for walkways will prevent the giant structure from being pulled apart by the glacier moving underneath it. It will be hermetically sealed within a shell of highly insulating panels.

Inside, they will be able to grow fresh salad crops. They expect to produce 20 kilograms of lettuce and cucumber each week of the winter season. The building will contain 150 private bedrooms, a well-equipped gymnasium and an aerobics studio.

The exceptionally clear, dry and stable atmosphere at the Pole will help scientists with their programmes. The Ice Cube, as the observatory is called, will detect neutrinos from outer space by lowering strings of light sensors down holes 2 kilometres deep in the ice. Scientists plan to use a new 10-metre telescope, operating at millimetre and submillimetre wavelengths, to study dark energy, the mysterious force believed to be responsible for the universe's accelerating expansion.

Key Points

1. Global warming may change Antarctica.
2. The question of exploiting Antarctica's resources will be a challenge for the Antarctic Treaty.
3. The USA is building a new centre at the Pole itself for new research projects.

The Ice Cube neutrino detector being built now at the Amundsen-Scott South Pole station in 2007.

An aerial view of the Amundsen-Scott South Pole station in February 2007. The wing of the Twin Otter aeroplane shows on the left.

Illustration credits

Alexander Turnbull Library: 8 (British Antarctic ["Terra Nova"] Expedition [1910–1913] Album), 20, 26 (British Antarctic ["Terra Nova"] Expedition [1910–1913] Album), 28t (British Antarctic ["Terra Nova"] Expedition [1910–1913] Album), 33, 40 (Norman Judd Collection), 42b (RNZAF Collection), 45t (British Antarctic Expedition 1901–04 Album), 46t, 49t (Shackleton Expedition, 1907–1909 Album), 50 (Joseph Kinsey Collection), 51, 53 (British Antarctic ["Terra Nova"] Expedition [1910–1913] Album), 54–57 (British Antarctic ["Terra Nova"] Expedition [1910–1913] Album), 66 (T O H Lees Collection), 67 (J Pontefract Album), 68, 70 (T O H Lees Collection), 71 (T O H Lees Collection), (British Antarctic ["Terra Nova"] Expedition [1910–1913] Album), 75, 76 (S C Smith Collection)

Canterbury Museum: 30, 34 (Angelo Collection), 35 (PJ Skellerup Collection), 37t, 37b, 38, 58, 59t, 61t, 61b (B Norris Collection), 62t (Quatermain Collection), 64, 74 (US Navy photograph), 78, 81 (J Weeber Collection), 83t, 83b (S McKay Collection), 85 (Quatermain Collection)

Library of Congress: 44 (George Grantham Bain Collection), 77 (George Grantham Bain Collection)

National Library of Australia: 49b (Sir Douglas Mawson Collection), 63t&b (Sir Douglas Mawson Collection), 73 (Sir Douglas Mawson Collection)

National Oceanic and Atmospheric Administration (NOAA): 9 (Commander John Bortniak, NOAA Corps), 10 (Archival photograph by Steve Nicklas), 16 (Michael Van Woert, NOAA NESDIS, ORA), 17 (Commander John Bortniak, NOAA Corps), 19 (Michael Van Woert, NOAA NESDIS, ORA), 22 (Jamie Hall), 23b (Michael Van Woert, NOAA NESDIS, ORA), 24t (Dave Mobley, Jet Propulsion Laboratory), 25b (Animals collection), 27 (Commander John Bortniak, NOAA Corps), 36 (Archival photograph by Steve Nicklas), 43 ((Michael Van Woert, NOAA NESDIS, ORA), 48, 59b (Archival photograph by Steve Nicklas), 60 (Archival photograph by Steve Nicklas), 82t&b (Dave Grisez)

New Zealand Herald: 92

New Zealand Post: 6

Holly Roach: 7, 12, 15, 21, 69

Southland Museum & Art Gallery: 9, 42t

Rob Suisted: page surrounds

US Antarctic Program/National Science Foundation: 11t (Emily Stone), 11b (Steve Roof), 13 (Scott Smith), 18t (Peter Recjek), 18b (Kurtis Bermeister), 23t (Peter Recjek), 25t (Jack Cummings), 28b (Scot Jackson), 29t (Michael Hoffman), 31t, 31b (Emily Stone), 45b (Dave Grisez), 46b (Dominick Dirksen), 47 (James Robert Washburn Jr), 79 (Commander Jim Waldron USNR [Retired]), 80 (Dave Grisez), 84 (Commander Jim Waldron USNR [Retired]), 87 (Rob Jones), 88 (Alexander Colhoun), 90 (Peter Recjek), 91 (Peter Recjek), 93 (Peter West), 94t&b (Alexander Colhoun), 95 (Kris Kuenning), 97t (Forest Banks), 97b (Scot Jackson), 104 (Emily Stone)

Index